"You Don't ~~tle~~ **te Practically Screamed The Words At Him. "I'm Not Sure You Ever Did."**

"That's not fair, Kate. I did know you once. And you knew me. We knew each other inside out." He reached out and lifted her hand, then placed it over his heart. "There was a time when I thought—" He dropped his hold on her as if her hand had suddenly become red-hot. "Sorry. Old habits die hard. Being with you brings back a lot of memories. Good memories."

Don't look back, she told herself. *Don't get sucked in by those good memories.*

It would be so easy to fall into Trent's arms, to fall into his bed in an effort to recapture what they'd once shared. But no matter what happened, even if they found their child, they couldn't go back. It was too late for them.

It was too late for *all* of them.

Dear Reader,

Welcome to another passion-filled month at Silhouette Desire. Summer may be waning to a close, but the heat between these pages is still guaranteed to singe your fingertips.

Things get hot and sweaty with Sheri WhiteFeather's *Steamy Savannah Nights*, the latest installment of our ever-popular continuity DYNASTIES: THE DANFORTHS. *USA TODAY* bestselling author Beverly Barton bursts back on the Silhouette Desire scene with *Laying His Claim*, another fabulous book in her series THE PROTECTORS. And Leanne Banks adds to the heat with *Between Duty and Desire*, the first book in MANTALK, an ongoing series with stories told exclusively from the hero's point of view. (Talk about finally finding out what he's *really* thinking!)

Also keeping things red-hot is Kristi Gold, whose *Persuading the Playboy King* launches her brand-new miniseries, THE ROYAL WAGER. You'll soon be melting when you read about Brenda Jackson's latest Westmoreland hero in *Stone Cold Surrender*. (Trust me, there is nothing cold about this man!) And be sure to *Awaken to Pleasure* with Nalini Singh's superspicy marriage-of-convenience story.

Enjoy all the passion inside!

Melissa Jeglinski

Melissa Jeglinski
Senior Editor
Silhouette Desire

Please address questions and book requests to:
Silhouette Reader Service
U.S.: 3010 Walden Ave., P.O. Box 1325, Buffalo, NY 14269
Canadian: P.O. Box 609, Fort Erie, Ont. L2A 5X3

USA TODAY Bestselling Author

BEVERLY BARTON

THE PROTECTORS

laying his claim

FROM THE LIBRARY OF CARMEN LOPEZ BUSTOS

Silhouette® *Desire*

Published by Silhouette Books

America's Publisher of Contemporary Romance

SILHOUETTE BOOKS

ISBN 0-373-76598-3

LAYING HIS CLAIM

This edition published by arrangement with Harlequin Books S.A.

® and TM are trademarks of Harlequin Books S.A., used under license.
Trademarks indicated with ® are registered in the United States Patent
and Trademark Office, the Canadian Trade Marks Office and in other
countries.

Visit Silhouette Books at www.eHarlequin.com

Printed in U.S.A.

BEVERLY BARTON

has been in love with romance since her grandfather gave her an illustrated book of *Beauty and the Beast*. After marriage to her own "hero" and the births of her daughter and son, Beverly chose to be a full-time homemaker, aka wife, mother, friend and volunteer. The author of over thirty-five books, Beverly is a member of Romance Writers of America and helped found the Heart of Dixie chapter in Alabama. She has won numerous awards and has made the Waldenbooks and *USA TODAY* bestseller lists.

To my children and grandchilden:
Badiema, Roger, Brant, Jana, Braden and Bryce.
And to my husband, Billy.
Life gives us no greater treasure
than the blessing of a family.

Prologue

The springtime sunshine shimmered through the stained-glass windows in the old Congregational church. Built in 1834 by Prospect, Alabama's wealthiest families, the magnificent brick structure had withstood the ravages of time, even the War Between the States, and with loving care and several restorations, stood today as not only a house of worship, but a historical treasure. Although she often felt out of place in the church her husband's family had helped establish, Kate attended services every Sunday with Trent and his aunt Mary Belle, Prospect's social grande dame and the bane of Kate's existence. It wasn't that Aunt Mary Belle was ever openly rude to Kate; the exact opposite was true. She smiled at her nephew's wife, patted her affectionately on the back and sung her praises to everyone within earshot. But in subtle ways the woman never let Kate forget that she wasn't quite worthy of Trenton

Bayard Winston IV and took it upon herself to continuously tutor Kate on the proper way to do absolutely everything.

Kate refused to allow Aunt Mary Belle to ruin this glorious Easter Sunday—Mary Kate's first Easter. She wanted the day to be perfect for her two-month-old daughter, the joy of her life. Despite the fact that Aunt Mary Belle had chosen both Kate's and Mary Kate's Easter frocks and decided on the luncheon menu, at least Kate had been allowed to put together her child's first Easter basket. Whenever she complained to Trent, asking him why they couldn't move out of the family mansion—another Prospect historical landmark that dated to the early part of the nineteenth century—he'd kiss and hug her and plead with her to be patient and understanding with his aunt.

"I know Aunt Mary Belle can be overbearing, but she means well," Trent had said numerous times. "This is my home—our home—as well as hers. She's like a mother to me. How could I ask her to leave? After all, she was born in this house and has lived here all her life. I grew up here and want to raise my children here, too."

So for nearly two years Kate had endured Aunt Mary Belle's overbearing guidance, but since Mary Kate's birth, the situation had grown worse. Although she never came right out and said as much, it was obvious that Aunt Mary Belle believed she and she alone should have the last word on how her great-niece was raised. For over two months now, Kate had smiled when she wanted to cry. She'd bitten her tongue to keep from lashing out and she'd agreed to things she hated, in order to keep peace in the family. But she had decided things simply had to change—and soon. She wanted a home of her own and this time when she told Trent she wanted them to move, she wouldn't let him sweet-talk her into staying. As much as she loved Trent—and she all but worshiped the ground he walked on—she could not live the rest of her life being treated at best like an ignorant child and at worst like a servant.

"Why don't we walk home from church today?" Kate suggested to Trent. "It's only a few blocks and it's such a beautiful day." She wanted time alone with her husband this afternoon so she could lead him by the cottage on Madison Avenue. The house had been empty for several years and although it needed some repairs, it was still a lovely home. The place consisted of a huge lot and the house itself was probably a good three-thousand square feet, large by most standards, although much smaller than Winston Hall, which boasted over ten-thousand square feet.

"Not today, Kate. You know Aunt Mary Belle has invited the minister and his family to dinner with us and—"

"Please, Trent. We won't be late for dinner. I promise."

"But we have the car here, today. Remember, you didn't want to ride with Aunt Mary Belle today, so we—"

"Send Guthrie back later this afternoon for your car. Please. This is important to me."

Trent grinned at her—his sexy smile always turned her inside out—then he slipped his arm around her waist. "Here, let me take Mary Kate. She'll get too heavy for you on the walk home."

Smiling, laughter bubbling up inside her, Kate snuggled close to Trent. Keeping Mary Kate secure on her hip, she stood on tiptoe and kissed her husband's cheek. If only talking him into purchasing the old Kirkendall

House on Madison proved half as easy as persuading him to walk home from church, all her dreams just might come true. Dreams of having a home of her own, a place that didn't make her feel as if she were living in a museum.

Just as Kate turned to hand Mary Kate to Trent, Aunt Mary Belle cleared her throat. "Public displays of affection aren't in good taste," she said quietly so only Trent and Kate could hear her.

Ignoring his aunt's comment, Trent turned to her and said, "Kate and I thought we'd walk home from church today. And you needn't worry about our being late for lunch. We won't keep Reverend and Mrs. Faulkner waiting."

"If you intend to walk, then how do you plan for me to get home. I have no desire to walk." Mary Belle laid her ring-adorned left hand over her heart and sighed dramatically.

"Why would you have to walk?" Kate asked. "Guthrie can—"

"I told Guthrie not to bother picking me up, that I'd ride home with y'all." Mary Belle smiled triumphantly.

Trent squeezed Kate around the waist. "We can't ask Aunt Mary Belle to walk, can we? She doesn't approve of ladies perspiring."

"I do not perspire," his aunt corrected him. "Ladies glow or glisten. They never perspire."

"Give Aunt Mary Belle the keys to your car," Kate suggested. "She can drive—"

"I'm unaccustomed to Trent's car and I do so hate to drive any vehicle, but when I'm forced to drive myself I prefer my own Lincoln."

"You could make an exception, just this once, couldn't you?" Kate had no intention of losing this battle. She had lost far too many during her marriage. Maybe she was being silly to make such a big deal out of this, but damn it—*oh, yes, excuse me, ladies don't curse, either, do they?*—she was sick and tired of Aunt Mary Belle running every aspect of her life.

"My dear Kate, is it so much to ask that an old lady, wearing high heels, not be forced to walk endless blocks on a warm Sunday afternoon? Or to be made uncomfortable by driving an unfamiliar car?"

Kate cringed. Trent chuckled. He adored his stuffy, snobby aunt and accepted everything she said and did with good humor. He'd once told Kate that he knew Aunt Mary Belle's many faults only too well and never took her too seriously. But he loved her. She had been both mother and father to him since his parents' untimely deaths when he was twelve.

Trent took his aunt's gloved hand. "Come along. We'll all ride home together. No need to fret." He glanced at Kate, who glared at him. "You and I will find time later today for a walk."

No we won't, Kate wanted to shout. *I will not compromise this time. Just this once, take my side. Please, Trent, don't let her win. Not again.*

"By all means, you go ahead and drive Aunt Mary Belle home. We certainly don't want to do anything that might displease her." Kate looked her husband square in the eyes, tilted her chin and gave him a tense smile. "Mary Kate and I are going to walk home." With that said, she turned and headed down the sidewalk.

"Kate," Trent called to her.

Ignoring him, she increased her pace and hurried away from him.

"Kate!"

Don't shout, dear, it's so unbecoming, Kate could almost hear Aunt Mary Belle scolding Trent. But she was too far away from them to actually hear their conversation. Various church members spoke to her, some nodded, and several, who had probably heard Trent calling her name, looked at her peculiarly. She nodded and smiled and kept on walking. Faster and faster.

Mary Kate whimpered. Kate slowed her pace, then halted to check on her daughter. "What's the matter, sweetheart?" Her baby girl looked up at her with big brown eyes identical to Trent's. "Is Mommy walking too fast? Or do you realize I'm upset?"

Mary Kate gurgled and cooed. Kate adjusted her child's hand-smocked pink bonnet. A large blond curl popped out from under the brim to lay against her forehead.

Kate walked down Third Street. Only two blocks until Madison. If she couldn't show her husband her dream house, at least she could show her daughter. And they'd take as long as they liked. She didn't care if they were late for lunch. Let Aunt Mary Belle gripe and grumble. Let Reverend and Mrs. Faulkner wait. And if Trent was upset with her, she didn't care.

The Kirkendall house was on a corner lot at the end of the four-hundred block of Madison. According to the Realtor Kate had spoken to about the property, the house was a Sears Roebuck structure built in 1924. Painted white, with green shutters, a gabled roof and a wide, wraparound porch, it wasn't anything fancy, just homey. A white picket fence encased the front yard. This was the kind of house Kate had always wanted.

"Look at that big front porch," Kate said to her baby. "We'll put a swing on that end and a couple of big rocking chairs. We can come out here and I'll rock you to sleep for your afternoon naps." Kate reached down, unlatched the front gate and walked down the brick sidewalk. "Look, sweetheart, there's a huge backyard. We'll get you a swing set and a playhouse and—"

"How'd do, ma'am," a woman's voice called out behind her.

Gasping at the sound of the unexpected voice, Kate whirled around and stared wide-eyed at the tall, rather gangly young woman not more than fifteen feet behind her. "Who—who are you?"

"Oh, dear, I'm sorry. I didn't mean to frighten you. But I'm new to Prospect. My husband and I are moving here from Birmingham and I happened to notice the For Sale sign."

Kate let out a relieved sigh. How silly of her to have overreacted, to have been momentarily frightened. Then the woman's comment registered in Kate's mind. This person was interested in the Kirkendall house. *No, please, this is my house. My husband and daughter and I are going to live here and be so very happy. You'll have to find yourself another house.*

"This house is really old and needs a lot of repairs. I'm sure you can find something you'd like much better," Kate said.

The woman wore jeans, a nondescript white blouse and white sneakers. Her hair was short and dark. And she wore sunglasses, which she didn't remove even when she walked into the shade as she approached Kate.

"Perhaps you're right. My husband would prefer something that we can move into without having to do any work." The woman reached out and touched Mary Kate's cheek. "She's beautiful. How old is she?"

"She'll be three months old the fourth of next month.."

"We're trying to have a baby, but…" The woman paused, then swallowed as if trying not to cry. "Would you mind if I hold her?"

Kate felt so sorry for this poor woman. What would it be like, she wondered, to want a child and be unable to have one? She'd gotten pregnant immediately as soon as she and Trent started trying.

"She's a bit of a mommy's girl," Kate said as she handed her daughter to the friendly stranger. "I'm Kate Winston and this is Mary Kate."

The woman took Mary Kate into her arms. "Sweet baby. Your mommy is so lucky to have you." She smiled at Kate. "I'm Ann Smith." She glanced at the house. "Are you the owner?"

"No, I'm not, but I have to admit that I'm interested in buying this house." Kate surveyed the house from the flight of concrete steps leading up to the porch, to the welcoming front door flanked by window panels and all the way up to the dormer roofline. "I'd hoped to show this house to my husband today and—"

Mary Kate whimpered loudly. Kate turned. The stranger was walking down the brick sidewalk toward the street. What did she think she was doing? Where was she going?

"Hey, you, come back here." Kate ran down the sidewalk. "Stop! Stop right this minute!" Was this poor woman trying to steal Mary Kate?

With her heart pounding like mad, Kate caught up with the woman just as she walked through the gateway. When she clamped her hand down on the woman's shoulder and reached out for Mary Kate, a large, strong hand grabbed her from behind and jerked her backward, away from the woman. Fighting fiercely, Kate was no match for the man who shoved her to the ground, then kicked her in the ribs. Kate balled up in pain and screamed.

"Get the kid in the car," the man shouted.

Yelling for help, crying out for her baby, Kate tried to stand, but the man knotted his hand into a fist and hit her several times, knocking her to her knees with the final punch. Her mouth and nose bled profusely. Pain radiated through her body, but she crawled up the sidewalk and watched helplessly as the woman got in the car with Mary Kate and the man jumped behind the wheel and sped off. Unable to maintain her balance, she fell over on her side.

"Oh, God, help me! Please, please!"

It didn't happen, she told herself. It couldn't possibly have happened. Not in Prospect, Alabama. And not to her. She was Mrs. Trenton Bayard Winston IV.

"Mary Kate…" Tears poured down her cheeks as she struggled to stand.

She heard people running, coming toward her. Then she heard voices. As she looked up from where she lay, unable to do more than lift her hand in a plea for help, she recognized Portia and Robert Meyer, who lived two houses down from the Kirkendall place.

"Mary Kate!" Kate called out her daughter's name. "They—they took my baby!"

One

"**H**ow long will you be staying, ma'am?" the hotel clerk, whose name tag read B. Walding, asked, a wide smile on his boyish face.

"I'm not sure," Kate replied. "A few days, possibly longer. I'm sorry I can't be more specific. Will it be a problem?"

"We aren't overbooked by any means," Mr. Walding told her. "We have more vacancies here at Magnolia House during the winter months and this being January, we're practically empty. Of course we fill up pretty quick over the holidays and in May, during Pilgrimage Week, we're always booked solid."

Oh, yes, she remembered Pilgrimage Week, one of Mary Belle Winston's favorite times, when Prospect's Junior League and the various garden clubs joined forces with the historical society to act as hostesses at the historical places in the little town and surrounding county. Aunt Mary Belle opened up Winston Hall to tourists and excelled in her role as mistress of the grand old estate. During her two-year marriage to Trent, Kate had been allowed to dress in costume, too, and assist Trent's aunt as a hostess. Kate had always felt out of place in the pantaloons and hoop skirt. Since she knew for a fact that her family had been poor dirt farmers for generations, she doubted any of her ancestresses had ever owned anything half so fine.

Kate shook off the memories, unsnapped her shoulder bag and removed her wallet. "I don't suppose y'all have room service, do you?"

The freckle-faced clerk grinned and shook his head. "No, ma'am, we don't. But if you want a plate lunch or a sandwich, I can run over to McGuire's and get something for you."

McGuire's. Best barbecue and ribs in southeast Alabama. She and Trent had often eaten at McGuire's when they'd been dating. "Is that place still open?"

"Sure is." Mr. Walding studied her closely. "You been to Prospect before, have you?"

"Yes. Years ago."

"Well, we're glad to have you back, Miss—?"

"Ms. Malone." Kate handed him her credit card. "Kate Malone."

"Ms. Malone, we're glad you're back in Prospect for a visit. You got folks hereabouts?"

"No, I— No I don't have any relatives here in Prospect." Not unless you counted an ex-husband and his aunt. Or a few of her stepfather's distant cousins.

"I can run over to McGuire's for you, if you'd like."

"Thanks, Mr. Walding, but I'll just pick up something later."

"Please, call me Brian." He zipped her credit card

quickly and returned it to her, then handed her a key. A real key. "Room one-oh-four. Want me to carry your bag for you?"

"No, thanks," Kate told him. "I travel light." She hoisted the vinyl carryall over her shoulder and glanced around the lobby.

"One-oh-four is to your right."

Kate smiled at the clerk. "Oh, by the way, Brian, does the Winston family still live at Winston Hall?"

"Do you know the family?"

"I knew Trent Winston."

Brian grinned. "I guess that Trent Winston knows every pretty girl who's ever lived in Prospect and at least half who've just passed through."

"Is that right?"

"Well, Ms. Malone, if you ever knew him…of course that depends on how long ago you knew him. But for the past ten years, he's been quite the man about town, if you know what I mean. Ever since his wife up and left him…" Brian leaned over the reception desk and lowered his voice. "Do you know about his wife and daughter?"

Kate's stomach knotted painfully. She shook her head, falsely denying any knowledge.

"I wasn't living here, then, mind you. I came here from Dothan about seven years ago. But it seems Trent Winston's baby daughter was kidnapped and his wife left him. Folks say his wife went kind of funny in the head after—"

"That's terrible about his wife and child," Kate said, not wanting to hear the local gossip about how she went crazy after Mary Kate was abducted. She knew only too well how close she came to a complete nervous breakdown. "Does Trent…does Mr. Winston and his aunt still live at Winston Hall?"

"Yes, ma'am. Miss Mary Belle still lives there and despite the stroke she had last year, she manages to oversee what little real society there is left in Prospect. And Mr. Trent's a circuit court judge now. Got elected by a landslide. Heck, every female in the county voted for him."

Keeping her smile in place, Kate quickly escaped from the chatty Mr. Walding and hurried down the corridor toward one-oh-four. After unlocking the door, she entered the small but rather elegant room. Magnolia House had been built at the turn of the century, and except for a dozen years in the early sixties to mid-seventies, had been open for business. Over thirty years ago the town had purchased the building and statewide investors, with a penchant for preserving history, had restored the old place. Most buildings and houses in Prospect were steeped in history, and keeping the past alive was important to a lot of people, but the only part of the past that mattered to Kate was eleven years and nine months ago. One particular Easter Sunday when Mary Kate Winston had been stolen from her mother's arms.

After laying her handbag and suitcase on the bed, Kate shed her black wool coat and hung it in the antique armoire which served as a closet. After all these years, it seemed odd to be back in the sleepy little Southern town where she'd been born and raised. Her father had been killed in Vietnam, leaving her mother a young widow with a child. When Kate was five, her mother had remarried a likable man named Dewayne Harrelson and Kate's childhood, though poverty-stricken, had been relatively carefree and happy. She'd loved growing up on her stepfather's farm and hadn't minded helping her mother with the never-ending chores. She'd

graduated from Prospect High at seventeen, as the vale-
dictorian, and earned a scholarship to the University of
Alabama. For a high school graduation gift, her parents
had given her an older-model car—a blue Chevy Im-
pala—that she knew they hadn't been able to afford.

During her junior year in college her mother had
died from pneumonia and six months later, her stepfather succumbed to congestive heart failure. Discov-
ering that her parents' farm was mortgaged to the hilt,
Kate had had little choice but to let the bank foreclose.
That last year at the University of Alabama had been a
lean one. She'd lived practically hand to mouth, worked
two part-time jobs and somehow managed to maintain
a grade point average that allowed her to graduate
summa cum laude.

At Christmas time of her senior year, her stepfather's elderly aunt Opal had invited her to spend the holidays with her family in Prospect. Kate made it more
than halfway home before her old car laid down and
died. She'd been on a lonely stretch of Highway 82, between Montgomery and Prospect, and almost in tears
when a sleek gunmetal-gray Jaguar pulled in behind her.
The minute Trenton Bayard Winston IV emerged from
the sports car, Kate's heart had stopped for a millisecond and then began beating ninety-to-nothing. Of
course she'd known who Trent Winston was. Everyone
in Prospect knew him. He was the heir to the Winston
fortune, a descendant of Prospect's founding fathers,
and a student at the University of Alabama's School of
Law. And everyone knew that when he graduated from
college that coming spring and passed the bar, he would
begin work at the local law firm of Winston, Cotten and
Dickerson. Trent's father, grandfather and great-grand-
father had been lawyers.

Trent had given her a ride home that cold December day, and not in her wildest dreams had she ever imagined that before the next Christmas, she would be Mrs. Trenton Bayard Winston IV.

The Congregational church chimes ringing the hour jerked Kate back from her distant past to her present. She walked across the room, pulled back the sheers and looked out the window. The view, although limited, allowed her to see directly across the street at the town square where the county courthouse presided over downtown Prospect. Looking left along Main Street, she saw Corner Drugs and to her right was the office that housed the *Prospect Reporter,* the weekly newspaper. And next door was the building, over a century old, that housed the Winston, Cotten and Dickerson law firm.

Mr. Trent's a circuit court judge now. Every woman in the county voted for him. The hotel clerk's comments echoed inside her head.

She supposed that after their divorce Trent had reverted back into the ladies' man he'd been before they married. And why shouldn't he have done just that? Every unmarried woman in Prospect and half the women at the university had nearly died of broken hearts when Trent married her. Looking back now, she wondered why he'd married her when he could have had any woman he'd wanted. She'd been crazy in love with him. So much so that even now, she was probably still halfway in love with him…despite everything that had happened between them. But she could not allow any leftover feelings for Trent to resurface. She wasn't there to rekindle their fiery romance. After all, apparently Trent hadn't loved her as much as he'd told her he did. Otherwise, Mary Kate's kidnapping wouldn't have ripped them apart the way it did.

Kate let the sheers fall back into place, then she turned and walked into the bathroom. She needed to freshen up before driving over to Winston Hall. Maybe the polite thing to do was telephone first, but she preferred a surprise attack. As she washed her hands, Kate chuckled. Even after all these years, she still thought of facing Mary Belle Winston as engaging in battle with the enemy. *That old woman isn't your enemy anymore,* she told herself. *She has no power over you.* But Aunt Mary Belle wouldn't be happy to see Kate, that she knew for certain. After drying her hands, she looked into the mirror. When she'd left Prospect eleven years ago, she'd been barely twenty-four; now she was thirty-five and no longer the young beauty Trent had proclaimed her to be. But she was attractive. And she was tough. She had the guts to face not only Aunt Mary Belle, but to look Trent in the eye and tell him she'd been right and he'd been wrong. Mary Kate wasn't dead. Their daughter was alive.

You can't tell him she's alive, Kate warned herself. Kate had no proof that Mary Kate was one of the three little girls who were abducted from southeast Alabama around the same time Mary Kate was. But all three baby girls had been sold to adoptive parents within one month of that fateful Easter Sunday. And all three had been approximately three to four months old when adopted.

Kate drank a glass of water. Her hand quivered ever so slightly. *Stay calm. Stay in control.* She retrieved her purse from the bed, removed her lipstick and compact, put on a fresh coat of hot-pink gloss and then powdered her face.

Perhaps she should eat supper first and fortify her body with some of McGuire's ribs. She hadn't eaten a bite since breakfast in Memphis early this morning. *Stop looking for excuses to delay the inevitable,* an inner voice chided.

She took her coat from the armoire, slipped into it and draped the straps of her handbag over her shoulder. Squaring her shoulders she marched out of her room, down the corridor and out the hotel's back entrance. Magnolia House's guests parked in the rear. When she got into the rental car—a white Mercury—she suddenly wished she could drive up to Winston Hall in her own car, her very expensive Mercedes. The purchase of that car had been Kate's one and only extravagance. She lived in a small duplex in Smyrna, outside of Atlanta. She bought her clothes off the rack and the only jewelry she owned consisted of a watch, a pair of small gold hoop earrings and a single gold bracelet. For the past ten years, most of the money she'd earned, first as an Atlanta policewoman and later an agent for the prestigious Dundee Private Security and Investigation firm, had been spent searching for Mary Kate. Even with all of the Dundee Agency's resources, she'd run into one dead end after another. It appeared that her daughter had disappeared off the face of the earth. But Kate had never given up hope, never allowed herself to think that her child might be dead.

Although the Deep South often had very mild winters, this winter wasn't one of them. Today's temperature had dropped into the low forties and the clouds had a look of rain about them. Cold winter rain, perhaps even sleet or ice. Kate turned up the heat in her rental car as she headed down Main Street. Before she realized what she was doing, she turned off on Madison and drove slowly by the old Kirkendall house. The house had been fully restored, with fresh paint on the exterior and a new white picket fence had replaced the dilapidated one. Heavy white wooden rockers and a large swing graced the front porch. A decorative Christmas wreath still hung on the front door, nearly three weeks after the holiday. Some lucky family had purchased Kate's dream house. Apparently whoever lived here loved the old place as much as she had and had restored it with tender care. Whatever family lived there, Kate hoped they were very happy. As happy as she had believed Trent and Mary Kate and she would have been.

Emotion lodged in her throat. She willed herself not to cry. Now was not the time for tears. When she saw Trent again, she had to be in full control of her emotions. And when she faced Aunt Mary Belle, she had to show the old biddy that she wasn't in the least bit intimidated by her.

"Goodbye, dream house," Kate whispered as she drove away from four-ten Madison.

In no time at all, she pulled up in front of Winston Hall, a magnificent Federal-style mansion that presided over almost a whole city block. The black iron fencing circled the estate and the massive black iron gates always stayed open, welcoming the elite of Prospect to come calling. And at holiday open houses and during Pilgrimage Week, even the lowly were allowed admittance. She'd forgotten how much she hated this house and how miserable her ex- husband's aunt had made her life for the two years of her marriage.

Don't look back, Kate reminded herself. *Nothing can change the past.*

She drove her rental car up and around the circular driveway, stopped directly in front of the mansion and killed the engine. After taking several deep breaths, she got out and walked up the steps and onto the porch. She checked her watch. Four-ten p.m. Too early for dinner. Kate smiled at the thought of her being invited to dine with the family.

She hesitated at the door, then garnered up all her courage and rang the bell. She barely recognized the elderly man who came to the door. His once-gray hair had turned white and his broad shoulders stooped just a little.

"Guthrie?"

"Yes, ma'am." His faded gray eyes focused on her face, studying her intently. "Miss Kate! That is you, isn't it? Lord have mercy, it's good to see you."

"Hello, Guthrie. How are you?"

"Tolerable," he replied. "You look mighty fine, Miss Kate. Hardly a day older than when you left here."

Kate laughed. She'd always been quite fond of Guthrie, who had worked for the Winston family since he'd been a boy. He served the household as a butler and a chauffeur and oversaw the other household staff, which when she'd lived there had consisted of a cook and a live-in maid for Mary Belle, and two daily maids who didn't live on the premises.

"I'm much older," Kate told him. "Ten years older."

"Been that long, has it?" As if suddenly realizing he'd kept her standing on the porch, Guthrie snapped to attention and said, "Come on in out of the cold, Miss Kate."

"Thank you." She entered the massive marble-floored foyer. When she glanced around, she noted that very little had changed. A spiral staircase took center stage in the room filled with antiques that had belonged to the family for generations.

"I never thought you'd come back," Guthrie said. "But Lord, have I prayed that you would. Mr. Trent, he's—"

"I've come to see Trent. Is he here?"

"Yes, ma'am, he's here. In his study." Guthrie looked up the stairs. "Miss Mary Belle's taking her Saturday afternoon nap."

Kate grinned. "Then perhaps I'll be fortunate enough to conduct my business with Trent and leave before she wakes."

Guthrie chuckled. "Shall I announce you to Mr. Trent or—"

"Since I no longer answer to the Good Manners Society—" Kate rolled her eyes toward the stairs "—why don't I just barge in on Trent without being announced?"

Guthrie chuckled again and gave Kate a wide, approving smile. "We've missed you, Miss Kate. We have missed you a great deal."

"Why thank you. I don't know what to say." And she truly didn't know how to respond to Guthrie's comment. *We have missed you,* he'd said. We? Surely he didn't mean Trent. Of course not. Trent was too busy being the man about town, wasn't he? Too busy charming all the ladies. But what if there's a special lady? What if he's found someone else? For all she knew, he could have remarried. But Mr. Walding at the Magnolia House hadn't mentioned anything about a new Mrs. Winston.

"Guthrie, Trent isn't…that is, has he remarried?"

"No, ma'am."

"Is he engaged?"

"No, ma'am. And you, Miss Kate?"

She shook her head. "No. Not married or engaged or anything."

Guthrie glanced down the hall in the direction of the library. "You know the way to Mr. Trent's study, don't you?"

She nodded.

"I do wish you were staying, ma'am."

He turned and walked away from her, down the hallway toward the kitchen, saving Kate from having to respond. The study, as Guthrie referred to the library at Winston Hall, was on the first floor, on the opposite side from the double parlors. When she reached the study, she found the door closed. Would the door be locked? she wondered. The only time Trent had ever locked the door was when the two of them had been alone in the study, making love. On the rug before the fireplace. On the massive Jacobean desk. On the leather sofa.

Don't do this to yourself. Stop remembering what it was like when you two were in love. But the memories washed over her like a tidal wave, sweeping away a decade of loneliness. And she had been lonely. So very lonely. She had dated a little in the past five or six years, a few really nice men, but try as she might, she hadn't come close to falling in love again. God knows she'd wanted to love someone, had prayed she'd find the courage to trust her heart to another man.

She lifted her arm, curled her right hand into a fist and knocked soundly on the closed door. Her heart fluttered maddeningly.

"Yes, come in," Trent said.

The sound of his deep, distinctive voice sent shock waves through her body. He had a slow, lazy, south Alabama drawl that had always seemed so sexy. But then again, everything about Trent Winston had been sexy. And probably still was.

Kate opened the door and took a hesitant step over the threshold. Trent sat in one of the massive oxblood leather armchairs in front of the fireplace so she could see only his left arm. He wore a cream sweater. Despite being modernized with central heat and air conditioning, Winston Hall kept a chill all winter. Old houses tended to be drafty.

"Hello, Trent." Her heartbeat thundered in her ears.

He didn't move, didn't speak.

"I apologize for not calling first, but I—I—"

Trent jumped to his feet abruptly and turned to face her. "Kate? Good God, it is you."

"Yes, it's me."

She stared at him. Blatantly. He had changed. Matured. His shoulders appeared broader. And there were lines around his eyes and mouth. A touch of gray mingled with the dark brown strands of his thick hair, mostly in his sideburns. He was still as handsome as ever, maybe even more so. Maturity certainly agreed with him. But then she'd always known he'd be a good-looking man in his forties and fifties, probably even in his eighties.

"What—when…it's been a long time," he finally managed to say.

"It's been ten years since our divorce became final."

"What brings you back to Prospect?" He hadn't moved an inch from where he stood by the leather chair.

"Personal business."

"I didn't realize you had any family still living here."

"I don't."

He studied her curiously, his dark, pensive brown eyes surveying her from head to toe. "You look—" He cleared his throat. "You look well. The years have been good to you."

"To you, too."

He took a tentative step toward her, then paused. "Please, come in. Would you care for a drink?" He indicated the bar set up on a serving cart stationed beneath one of the two massive floor-to-ceiling windows on the side wall.

"No, thanks." She ordered her feet into action and managed to walk toward him.

With their gazes locked, they met in the middle of the room, each stopping when less than three feet separated them. She could barely suppress the urge to reach out and touch him. They stood there for an endless moment, neither moving nor speaking.

"You said you're in Prospect on personal business. Since you've come to Winston Hall, am I to assume that business concerns me in some way?"

"Yes, it concerns you." *Don't drag this out. Dammit, just tell him.* "I work for the Dundee Agency. It's a private security and investigation firm based in Atlanta."

"You're a private investigator?"

Trent grinned and her stomach did a crazy flip-flop.

"Yes. And before I worked at Dundee's, I was an Atlanta police officer."

Trent shook his head. "You must have changed a great deal. I can't imagine my sweet Kate as either a policewoman or a P.I."

His sweet Kate? *Dammit, Trent, I haven't been your sweet Kate in a long, long time.*

"Recently, a colleague and I were sent to Maysville, Mississippi, a town about an hour's drive from Memphis," she told him. "A two-month-old baby boy had been kidnapped and my colleague was the child's father."

Trent's face paled. "You work on child abduction cases?"

"On this one, yes. I went to Maysville with the kidnapped baby's father and helped him and the child's mother through some difficult days."

"What happened to the baby?" Trent's jaw tightened.

"He was rescued," Kate said. "And returned to his parents."

"That's good." Trent turned away from her. "I'm happy for them."

"The FBI agent working on the case was the head of a sting operation that the bureau had in the works for several years," Kate explained. "You see, there was an infant abduction ring working in the southeast and these people had been stealing babies for the past twelve years."

Trent whirled around and glared at her. "Damn, Kate, don't tell me you've somehow convinced yourself that Mary Kate was taken by the same abduction ring." He came toward her, fury in his eyes. He grabbed her by the shoulders and shook her gently. "I had hoped that after all this time you would have accepted the fact that our little girl is lost to us forever."

Kate gritted her teeth in an effort to stem the tide of tears gathering in her eyes. "Dante Moran was the FBI agent in charge of the operation. He's an objective professional, someone without any connection to Mary Kate. He—he believes that there's a very good possibility that our daughter could be one of three baby girls stolen from southeast Alabama the same month and year that Mary Kate was taken."

After loosening his tenacious hold on her shoulders, Trent narrowed his gaze and glowered at Kate.

"There are hundreds of children who were sold to desperate adoptive parents during the past twelve years," Kate said. "These people, the ones in charge of the abduction ring, kept a file on each infant. The state and sometimes even the city where the child was abducted was noted on records, as was the month the child was supposedly given up for adoption. The FBI is in the process of notifying the adoptive parents of every stolen child, and they're searching for all possible birth parents, too."

"And this FBI agent, this Mr. Moran, believes Mary Kate is one of these children?" Trent gripped Kate's shoulders with gentle force.

She nodded. "There are three eleven-year-old girls who were taken by this abduction ring as infants from this area of Alabama, and given to adoptive parents within a month after Mary Kate was taken. The FBI has already pulled a copy of Mary Kate's birth certificate and the next step is to give the FBI lab a DNA sample. Then they'll compare it to a sample they will take from each of these girls."

Trent caressed Kate's shoulders. "And if none of these little girls turn out to be Mary Kate, what will you do then? Will you finally give up and let her go?"

"Please, Trent, try to believe in the possibility that Mary Kate is alive and we could find her and—"

"And what? Even if by some miracle one of these girls is Mary Kate, what would we do? Rip her away from two loving parents, perhaps from brothers and sisters? And if we did, what do we have to give her— divorced parents fighting over custody?" Trent released Kate and stomped across the room. "No. I don't want to hear this. My daughter is dead. She's been dead for eleven years."

"Don't say that. Mary Kate is alive. And I'm going to find her. I came here hoping you'd want to go with me to find our little girl. But I see now what a terrible mistake I made. I'm sorry I bothered you."

Kate ran from the study and down the hall, not stopping when Trent called her name. Tears blurred her vision as she rushed outside and hurried to her rental car. She got in, started the engine and headed down the driveway. When she reached the street, she glanced in her rearview mirror and saw Trent standing on the porch, his arms crossed over his chest.

Two

Kate prepared herself a cup of hot tea. She always carried a box of Earl Grey with her whenever she traveled, which in her line of business was most of the time. Wearing her raspberry-pink cotton flannel robe over matching pajamas, she walked out of the bathroom and over to one of two lounge chairs flanking the small table near the windows. After placing the white mug with the Magnolia House emblem—appropriately a magnolia blossom—on the table, she picked up the TV remote control and flipped on the one local station. She hit the Mute button to silence the commercial's chatter, then eased down into the chair and propped her feet on the edge of the nearby bed. Her stomach growled, reminding her that she hadn't eaten any supper. But she'd been so upset, so damn angry when she left Winston Hall, that she wouldn't have been able to keep a bite of food down if she had eaten.

My daughter is dead. She's been dead for eleven years. Trent's words echoed inside her head…inside her heart.

His firm conviction that Mary Kate was dead and her equally resolute certainty that their child was still alive had been the single major issue that finally ended their marriage. Of course it hadn't helped that they'd both blamed themselves for their child's abduction or that she'd suffered a nervous breakdown at the time. And Mary Belle Winston's constant interference had only added fuel to the fire that destroyed any hope of them being able to salvage their relationship.

Why had she bothered coming back to Prospect? What had she been thinking? She should have known that even bringing Trent news of what she considered a miracle wouldn't sway him from his stubborn stand. *How could he not want to find Mary Kate?* She didn't understand his reasoning. But then, she never had.

Dante Moran had given her the basic facts which led her to believe that Mary Kate was one of the girls who'd been adopted over eleven years ago. Even Moran thought it was highly likely. And his was an objective opinion. *So why couldn't Trent believe? Why couldn't he open up his heart to the possibility?*

A fierce ache gripped Kate's chest, emotion so deep and powerful that it took her breath away. Mary Kate *was* alive. She'd always know in her heart of hearts that her baby girl wasn't dead. Now, within a few weeks, she might see Mary Kate, touch her, hold her, tell her that she loved her.

Once again Trent's words tormented Kate. *Even if by some miracle one of these girls is Mary Kate, what would we do? Rip her away from two loving parents, perhaps from brothers and sisters? And if we did, what do we have to give her—divorced parents fighting over custody?*

Needing to comfort herself, Kate lifted her feet off the bed and drew her knees up toward her chest, then hugged her arms around her legs in a fetal gesture. Since the moment Dante Moran had shared the FBI's information with her about the abduction ring's confidential files, she'd dreamed of the moment she would hold her child in her arms again. And she had pushed every negative thought to the back of her mind. But Trent had reminded her of the reality of the situation. Mary Kate wouldn't know her, wouldn't think of Kate as her mother. Her daughter would have been raised by other people. She might already have a mother and father she loved. Where would Kate fit into Mary Kate's life?

Kate keened mournfully, the sound little more than a whimper. Oh, God, her little Mary Kate wouldn't be Mary Kate. Her adoptive parents would have given her another name.

What do we have to give her—divorced parents fighting over custody?

Get out of my mind, damn you, Trent, she screamed silently.

Wouldn't it be enough to know that her daughter was alive? Wouldn't it be enough to see her? she asked herself. *It should be enough. But would it be?*

Special Agent Moran had pointed out that this case would turn into a legal nightmare once all the adoptive parents were informed their children had been stolen from their biological parents and not given up freely. Both sets of parents would have rights. Lawyers would be hired. Court battles would be fought, won and lost.

What would she do if she found that Mary Kate was

a happy child, living with loving parents and perhaps even had siblings? *Stop it! Don't keep torturing yourself this way.* She could make those kinds of decisions later, after she knew for sure that one of the little girls actually was her daughter. First things first..

Sighing, Kate picked up her mug and took several swallows of the delicious tea. Ah, how soothing, how warming. Odd that although she'd never drank anything except iced tea until she married Trent, once Aunt Mary Belle had introduced her to the delicate, distinct taste of Earl Grey, she'd become a lifelong convert. Looking back, she had to admit that all her memories of her ex-husband's overbearing aunt weren't bad. And as much as she had resented the woman's constant tutelage, she had learned a great deal from the old biddy.

Why waste time thinking about that woman? Kate wouldn't have to see her or speak to her. At least she'd been spared that much on this trip. She would leave Prospect first thing in the morning and go straight back to Memphis, where the investigation into finding the birth parents of hundreds of kidnapped children was in full swing. Trent could do as he pleased. She'd done her duty—she'd informed him about the situation.

Just as she began to relax—the aftereffects of the hot bath she'd taken a few minutes ago, the soothing tea and the comfy clothes—someone knocked at her hotel door. Trent? Damn, why was he the first thing that popped into her mind. Wishful thinking?

Kate stood, walked across the room and peered through the peephole. Mary Belle Winston! The last person on earth she ever wanted to see again. Damn. Double damn.

Go away, old woman, and leave me the hell alone. I don't want to talk to you.

Kate hesitated. Mary Belle knocked on the door repeatedly. Good grief, why wouldn't she go away?

"Katherine, I know you're in there," Mary Belle said. "I spoke to the desk clerk and he informed me that Ms. Malone was definitely in her room."

Blast! She'd have to speak to Brian Walding! How dare he give out any information about her, least of all her room number. But then considering who Mary Belle was in this town, he'd probably felt he had little choice. Either kowtow to the grande dame or risk losing his job.

After breathing in deeply and exhaling slowly, she squared her shoulders, stood straight and tall, and then said a please-God-help-me prayer before opening the door. "Hello, Miss Mary Belle."

"May I come in?"

Kate looked at Trent's aunt, really looked at her and was surprised by how much she had aged in the past eleven years. She no longer colored her hair so it was now a stunning snow-white. Delicate wrinkles lined her face, especially around her eyes and mouth. Never a beautiful woman, but always extremely well-groomed and attractive, Mary Belle still maintained that air of old south elegance few women could pull off in this day and time. Kate's gaze traveled from the older but familiar face to the ever present pearls that had belonged to Mary Belle's grandmother. And then Kate saw the cane.

"All right, come on in." Kate stepped aside to allow the woman entrance.

When Mary Belle entered the room, Kate noticed how heavily she braced herself on the cane, her steps slow and precise. What was it that Mr. Walding had said? Something about Mary Belle still presiding over Prospect society despite the stroke she'd had this past year?

"Not a very gracious response," Mary Belle said as she walked over and sat down in one of the two lounge chairs. "Your reply should have been 'yes, Miss Mary Belle, please come in.' And then you should have said—"

"Don't lecture me!" Kate slammed the door.

"I see you haven't changed," Mary Belle said.

Kate faced her nemesis. "And neither have you." Kate stomped across the room, acid churning in her stomach.

"That's where you're wrong, my dear." Mary Belle looked up, focusing her keen dark eyes on Kate. "Perhaps superficially I'm unchanged. I still do my best to rule Prospect society and I'm still an opinionated, domineering old maid who meddles in her nephew's life. But I'm now capable of admitting when I'm wrong and—" she took a deep breath "—I was wrong about you, Kate."

Kate stared at Trent's aunt, wary of her solicitous comment, suspicious of Mary Belle saying she was wrong about anything, especially Kate. "Why are you here? What do you want?"

Mary Belle sighed. *Still dramatic, too,* Kate thought.

"Those are my questions precisely," Mary Belle said. "Why are you here in Prospect, after so many years? And what do you want with Trent?"

"Didn't he tell you?" Kate flopped down in the other lounge chair and crossed her arms over her chest. She wanted to get this visit over with as quickly as possible.

"Trent told me nothing. I wouldn't have known you'd paid him a visit had I not been looking out my bedroom window when you left. I recognized you immediately, of course, and summoned Guthrie. He said you'd visited Trent, but stayed only a few minutes and that Trent stormed out of the house and drove off somewhere directly after you left. So, I assumed that he—"

"Followed me?" Kate laughed sarcastically. "Were you afraid he'd come after me and I might manage to get my hooks back into him?"

"You're terribly bitter, aren't you?" Mary Belle shook her head sadly. "Of course I don't blame you. But I had hoped that after all these years your anger at us— at me in particular—might have lessened."

Utterly confused by Mary Belle's comment, Kate glared at the old woman. "Look, Trent didn't follow me. He's not here. And I have no intention of seeing him again before I leave Prospect in the morning."

"That's a pity."

Kate shook her head in bewilderment. "Am I supposed to know what you mean by that?"

"No, probably not." Mary Belle leaned forward toward Kate. "I can think of only one reason you'd ever come back to Prospect—you've learned something about our precious Mary Kate's fate, haven't you?"

Kate swallowed the knot of emotion threatening to choke her. Despite all her faults, Trent's aunt had, as far as Kate was concerned, possessed one redeeming quality—she had loved Mary Kate and been devoted to the child. Selflessly devoted.

"I came here to give Trent some information about the possibility that it's only a matter of a few days before Mary Kate's whereabouts are known."

Mary Belle gasped. "Then she—she is alive?"

"Yes, I believe she is. I've never thought she was dead."

"Please, my dear, tell me everything."

Kate relayed the information to Trent's aunt, who sat there spellbound while Kate talked. Tears glistened in

Mary Belle's brown eyes. She blinked several times, then reached inside her coat pocket and retrieved a lace handkerchief. After lowering her glasses, she wiped her eyes.

"If I know my nephew—and I do—he stubbornly refused to believe there's a chance one of these little girls is our Mary Kate. And he probably even said that even if one of them was his child, it was too late to make her a part of his life again."

Kate nodded. "You do know him well, don't you?"

"He'll change his mind."

"I doubt it. Trent never changes his mind. Once he decides on something, he—"

"He's still stubborn, but not quite as bullheaded as he used to be. And he's no longer as arrogant and self-centered as he once was." Mary Belle reached across the table and grasped Kate's hand. "Losing Mary Kate... and losing you changed him. In some ways for the better, but in other ways, for the worse. But take my word for it, he will change his mind about wanting to find out if one of these girls is his daughter."

Kate snatched her hand away, then before she thought through her response, she said, "I'll give you my cell phone number, so if Trent wants to get in touch with me, he can." *How stupid was that?* her inner voice asked. *You don't want to see him again; don't want to feel physically or emotionally drawn to a man who hates you.* The last thing she needed was Trent Winston back in her life under any circumstances. She'd done what she thought was right—given him the information. If he chose to continue believing their daughter was dead...

"I'll go now," Mary Belle said. "I appreciate your talking to me. I would have understood if you'd slammed the door in my face."

When Mary Belle rose to her feet, slowly and awkwardly, Kate stopped herself from offering to help the old woman. Bearing her weight on the cane, Mary Belle walked toward the door. Kate stood and followed her.

When Mary Belle reached the door, she turned to face Kate. "Regardless of what Trent does…if it turns out that I'm wrong about him getting involved—would you…please…let me know what happens. If Mary Kate is alive, I'd very much like to know."

Willing herself not to cry, Kate nodded as unshed tears stung her eyes and nose. "You do understand that you have no legal right to interfere in any decisions I make about my daughter, don't you?"

"Kate, all I want is to know if she's alive. Even if I never see her—" Mary Belle's voice cracked. "Just a phone call…one phone call. That's all I ask. You don't have to give me any details."

"All right. If one of these girls is Mary Kate, I'll let you know."

"Thank you, my dear."

Kate opened the door. Mary Belle walked out and into the corridor and kept going, not once looking back. Her steps were very slow. Just as the old woman neared the end of the short hallway, Kate caught a glimpse of Guthrie taking her arm and leading her away. With a heavy sigh, Kate went back into her room and closed the door.

What the hell had just happened?

Had Mary Belle actually mellowed with age? Had she changed so much that Kate thought she might actually like Trent's aunt? Or had she been putting on an act, playing nice-nice in order to get what she wanted? What difference did it make? Mary Belle had no control over her. Kate didn't have to jump through hoops to please her, not ever again.

Kate turned off all the lights in the room, except the one on the nightstand, then she slipped out of her robe, tossed it into one of the lounge chairs and spread out sideways across the bed. She rested there, out from under the covers, her gaze riveted to the ten-foot ceiling. With her eyes wide open memories flashed through her mind. Memories she wanted to forget.

The first time Trent and she made love. Her expensive, elaborate wedding, coordinated by Aunt Mary Belle. Her pleas with Trent to move out of Winston Hall and into a home of their own. The day Mary Kate was born. Love. Happiness. Frustration. So many emotions swirled about inside her. The day her daughter was kidnapped. Fear. Anger. Anguish.

She lay there, mired in self-pity, her mind filled with memories, her heart breaking as if only today her world had fallen apart and she had lost her child and the only man she'd ever loved. She seldom allowed herself to have a case of poor-old-Kate, but just this once, she thought she was due—maybe overdue.

Trent drove his old Jaguar at demonic speed along the back roads of Bayard County. He seldom got behind the wheel of this classic car because it brought back too many memories of his life with Kate. Damn her for returning to Prospect. He'd spent over ten years trying to wipe her memory from his mind and had halfway convinced himself that he'd done just that. It had taken him a long time to forgive her and even longer to forget her and move on with his life. Only recently had he even considered the possibility of remarrying. He had avoided serious relationships as if they were a plague. But after dating Molly Stoddard for the past year, he'd convinced himself that she was the type of woman he needed. A woman from a well-to-do old Eufala family, a lawyer who had relocated to Prospect with her two children after her husband's untimely death three years ago and who now worked in Trent's family's firm. They had a great deal in common, knew all the same people, enjoyed many of the same things. And he liked her children, eight-year-old Seth and ten-year-old Lindy.

But you aren't in love with Molly, he reminded himself tonight, as he'd done repeatedly during the past few weeks, every time he thought about proposing to her. As far as he was concerned it was better for Molly and him that they weren't in love. They cared for each other, respected each other and shared a true friendship. He'd been so crazy in love with Kate that she had consumed him completely. He'd never felt about another woman the way he'd felt about her. And look how badly that had ended. They had hurt each other unbearably. He had disappointed her, had let her down and she'd ripped the heart right out of him when she left.

God help him, it still hurt. Hurt like hell. He wanted to think he was indifferent to Kate, that she meant nothing to him now. But the memories wouldn't hurt so damn bad unless he still felt something for her. So what did he feel for Kate? Anger. Distrust. Most definitely. But the sexual attraction that had once been so powerful between them was still there, at least on his part. He'd like to deny it, but he couldn't. Okay, so part of what he was feeling was just good old-fashioned lust. He could deal with that, couldn't he? Yeah, sure. All he had to do was avoid Kate.

But what about your daughter? What about Mary Kate? a tormenting inner voice asked. She's dead, he told himself. He shouldn't let Kate's enthusiasm affect him. Just because she believed a little girl who'd been kidnapped by some child abduction ring as an infant was Mary Kate, didn't make it so. Let Kate believe in miracles, let her cling to the dream that their child was still alive and they'd someday be reunited with her. He couldn't share that dream. For him that dream was a nightmare. He'd realized a few months after Mary Kate was stolen from them that the only way he could function, the only way he could survive and not fall apart completely was to let go of his daughter. Everyone involved in Mary Kate's kidnapping case—from local and state law enforcement to the FBI—had told them the odds were that they'd never see their child again, that if she hadn't been found within a month or less, they had to stop hoping, consider her lost to them forever and move on. He'd done that. Kate hadn't. In a way, his ex-wife had been far stronger than he, even if she had suffered an emotional breakdown. Even now, after all this time, she clung to the hope that she would find their daughter.

Trent hadn't been able to tell Kate eleven years ago that the reason he chose not to hope, chose to relinquish the dream of being reunited with Mary Kate, was because he didn't have the courage to face each new day with the agonizing questions of where their child was, what was happening to her, if she was being taken care of or being abused. He'd chosen the easiest route to recovery by convincing himself that their baby girl was dead.

What if Kate's right? What if the FBI locates Mary Kate? Didn't he want to see his daughter? Didn't he want to know firsthand that she was well and happy and loved?

Trent's cell phone rang. He slowed the Jag, removed the phone from its holder and punched the On button. "Trenton Winston."

"She's at the Magnolia House," his aunt Mary Belle said. "I made some inquiries to find out if she was still in town. She is. But I suggest you go see her tonight. My guess is she'll be gone by morning."

Before he could reply, his aunt hung up on him. Damn infuriating woman! How did she even know Kate was in Prospect? Had Guthrie told her that Kate had come to Winston Hall? Or had she seen Kate when she arrived or when she left? Aunt Mary Belle knows, he told himself, she knows Mary Kate may be alive. If she knew, that meant she'd talked to Kate. God help us all. What had it been like when those two had met again face-to-face?

Trent realized what he wanted to do, what he had to do. Deny it all he liked, the bottom line was that if his daughter was still alive, he had to know. He was older now, maybe a little wiser and a heck of a lot tougher than he'd been eleven years ago. Whatever happened, he could handle it and maybe this time he could actually help his wife—make that his ex-wife—through whatever lay ahead for them. He owed her that much, didn't he? He'd failed her miserably in the past.

Twenty minutes later, Trent parked his Jag in the rear parking area, got out, locked his car and headed for the Magnolia House's back entrance. When the cold night wind chilled his face, he flipped up the collar on his suede jacket. He swung open the hotel's back door, then walked down the hall and into the lobby area. He didn't know the clerk by name, although his face looked familiar.

"Good evening," Trent said.

"Good evening, Judge Winston," the man replied.

"I believe you have a Ms. Kate Malone staying here."

"Yes, we do. She's in room one-oh-four."

Trent eyed the man whose name tag read B. Walding. "I thought y'all weren't allowed to give out guests' room numbers."

"Ordinarily we're not," Mr. Walding said. "But since Ms. Malone is your ex-wife and you're who you are and all…well, it's like Miss Mary Belle said—"

"So my aunt has been here to see Kate…to see Ms. Malone?"

"Yes, sir. She left about thirty minutes ago and she did mention on her way out that you'd probably be stopping by to see your wife…your ex-wife.'"

Trent nodded, offered Mr. Walding a weak smile and glanced around trying to decide which corridor led to one-oh-four.

"To your right," the clerk told him.

"Thanks."

Nervous and unsure of how Kate would react to him just showing up, Trent marched down the hall. When he stood outside the door to one-oh-four, he hesitated. Once he knocked on the door, there would be no turning back.

He knocked several times. No response. He knocked again, harder this time.

He heard the sound of movement from inside the room, then footsteps. The door flew open and Kate stood there in a pair of baggy, bright pink pajamas, her long blond hair disheveled and her face void of makeup. And heaven help him, she was the sexiest thing he'd ever seen.

She stared up at him with those big, sky blue eyes of hers and his stomach knotted painfully. He remembered only too well how he'd felt the first time she'd zeroed those baby blues in on him. He'd gotten an instant hard-on. If he'd been honest with himself at that moment, he'd have known he was a goner. He'd never wanted anything as much as he'd wanted Kate Malone.

"I want to go with you to find Mary Kate," he told her.

She stared at him, an incredulous expression on her face. "You want to...are you telling me that you now believe there's a good chance our daughter is still alive?"

"I don't know what I believe," he admitted. All he knew was that he didn't want Kate to go through this alone. But he could hardly tell her that. She might read more into a statement like that than he intended. "We can be civil to each other, can't we? We can do this together as Mary Kate's parents and not as..." Trent shuffled his feet. "There's no need for us to hurt each other any more than we already have."

"I agree." As if suddenly realizing she'd been staring at him, Kate cleared her throat, glanced away and then said, "Meet me here in the morning at eight o'clock. If we can take your car, I'll turn my rental in and we can ride to Memphis together."

He nodded, then turned to leave. Sensing her watching him, he glanced over his shoulder. She stood in the doorway, temptation personified. Spending days, perhaps weeks with her was going to be pure torture for him. "Thanks, Kate," he said before walking away hurriedly, knowing that if he'd stayed another minute, he would have pulled her into his arms and kissed her.

Three

Kate hadn't slept much and felt the effects of a restless night. Knowing she needed some fortification to be at her best this morning, she'd eaten a substantial breakfast and downed three cups of regular coffee at the Prospect Café. When she paid the bill and left, she breathed a sigh of relief. Lucky for her, no one had recognized her. Apparently the local gossip mill hadn't processed the news that Trent Winston's ex-wife was in town. The café was a block from the hotel, so she'd walked the distance, despite the frigid temperature. The clouds that had falsely predicted a cold rain late yesterday had dissipated overnight and today promised to be sunny. The early morning sun shining brightly did little to warm things up. When she stepped out of the café, Kate slipped-on her red leather gloves and tightened the red wool scarf around her neck.

As she approached the Magnolia House, she checked

her watch. It was 7:53 a.m. Would Trent show up? Of course he would. If he hadn't already been certain of what he planned to do, he'd never have come to see her last night. While she'd tossed and turned during the long, seemingly endless night, she had been unable to turn off her mind, to stop a hundred and one thoughts from bombarding her. Memories of the past mixed and mingled with the present and unrealistic dreams for the future. If dreams came true, what would she want? She'd want to be a mother to Mary Kate. That was a given. But what about being a wife to Trent? Perhaps, in the deepest recesses of her heart, that dream existed.

Dreams were well and good. In their place. But she had to face reality. The odds were against her. Even if they found Mary Kate, Trent was right—it was too late to be the child's parents. Could she accept that fact? She really had no other choice. She had to accept the hard, cold facts in order to protect her daughter. One thing she knew for certain—the only thing that mattered was Mary Kate.

A late-model black Bentley pulled up at the front of the Magnolia House just as Kate crossed the street. She instantly recognized the driver. Right on time. Actually a few minutes early. Trent emerged from the car, looked in her direction and threw up his hand. She waved back at him, but forced herself not to increase her pace. She had run to him, into his open arms, countless times in the past, always striving to please him. But no longer. She wasn't the girl she'd once been. Time and circumstances had changed her dramatically.

When she drew closer, Trent came toward her, and they both stopped in the middle of the sidewalk. She offered him a cordial, halfhearted smile. "I've already checked out and put my bag in the rental car," she told him. "If you'll follow me to—"

"That won't be necessary," Trent said. "Guthrie will take care of your rental car later. We'll leave the keys with the clerk at the hotel." He cupped her elbow. "Why don't you give me the keys and I'll get your bag and give the keys to the clerk? You can wait here for me." He opened the front passenger door of his car.

Mr. Take-charge. Trent's trademark. During their brief marriage, he'd made all the decisions and she'd allowed him to, with very little protest. *Do not pick a fight with Trent first thing. Choose your battles. This issue is not worth arguing about and you know it.*

She unzipped her leather purse, retrieved the car keys and handed them to Trent. "Thanks." Avoiding direct eye contact with him, she got in the Bentley and closed the door.

The car had a luxurious feel. Real tan leather and real wood. It seemed odd that Trent, who loved his sports cars dearly, would be driving this sedate sedan. This was a family car, not a bachelor's wheels. Maybe this was Aunt Mary Belle's car. No, probably not. She doubted that his aunt was driving these days, not after her stroke. Besides, she'd always preferred to be chauffeured around by Guthrie.

A few minutes later, Trent returned, opened the trunk and placed her suitcase inside, then he got into the Bentley and glanced at Kate. "Ready?"

"Yes."

"You've had breakfast?" he asked.

"Yes. At the Prospect Café."

"Then we're set until lunchtime." He inserted the key and started the engine. "Do you have a route preference?" he asked. "It's close to an eight-hour trip whether we go through Tupelo or Decatur."

She laughed spontaneously, surprised that he'd asked her opinion. The man was certainly a contradiction these days. Part old Trent, part new Trent.

He eyed her quizzically.

"You're driving," she said. "You choose."

He nodded, then pulled the Bentley into the flow of the sparse morning traffic. "If at anytime during the next few days—or however long this takes—I become over-bearing and insufferable, feel free to hit me between the eyes with a two-by-four."

Kate smiled. At least this new Trent had retained the old Trent's sense of humor. "I'll keep that in mind. And don't be surprised if I do as you suggested. You see, I'm not the easily manipulated, naive, love-sick fool I was when we got married."

"You might have been naive and in love, but you were never a fool." Trent kept his gaze focused on the road. "And as I recall there were times when neither I nor Aunt Mary Belle could bring you around to our way of thinking."

Kate's smile vanished as she remembered how trag-ically her Easter Sunday rebellion nearly twelve years ago had ended.

"Don't go there," he told her. "I was not referring to that Easter Sunday. I seem to recall more than one oc-casion when you balked at being bossed around."

"I'm sure you and I remember the past differently."

"Some things, perhaps, but…"

"But what?"

"Nothing. I think we're better off not discussing the past. We're less likely to argue if we stick to the pres-ent. Don't you agree?"

"If that's what you want. Believe me, dredging up the past isn't something I enjoy."

While he kept his gaze focused directly ahead and both of them stayed quiet, Kate studied Trent. He was remarkably handsome. He came close to being a pretty boy, but wasn't. Not quite. His nose was a little too prominent, his mouth a little too wide. Age had given him an air of distinction, the kind old money and privilege could give a man approaching forty.

"How long have you been a circuit court judge?" she asked, breaking the silence.

"Five years."

"Do you like being a judge?"

"Yes, I do."

"Wasn't it a problem for you to take time off from work to come with me?"

"I arranged for another judge to take my cases for the time being. I consider this a family emergency." Trent cast her a sidelong glance. "What about you? Can you afford to take time off from work? If not, I can help you financially."

"Don't do me any favors." The words were out of her mouth before she realized it. "Sorry. I didn't mean to snap. Looks like I'm still sensitive about money issues. Your aunt Mary Belle often intimated that I'd married you for your money."

"She knows better," Trent said. "She knew better at the time. Any idiot could see how much in love we were. It wasn't a one-sided thing and everyone knew it. Even Aunt Mary Belle."

A zinging warmth spread quickly through Kate. Hearing Trent say in such a matter-of-fact way that he'd been so very much in love affected her deeply. She had believed he loved her—up until the day Mary Kate was abducted. From that time on, he'd given her numerous reasons to doubt his love.

"I don't need any financial help, but thank you for offering."

"Then your job as an investigator pays well?"

"Yes, it pays very well."

Silence.

Kate's heartbeat drummed softly in her ears. The well-insulated Bentley kept the outside noises to a minimum. How was it that this man she had once loved beyond all reason, who'd been her husband, her lover and her friend, now seemed like a stranger? Because that's what he is, she reminded herself. *Just as I'm a stranger to him. I'm no more the same person I was than he is.* Losing not only Mary Kate, but each other, both Trent and she had come through the ordeal with numerous battle scars. And in the years in between, they'd gone their separate ways and built new lives.

"You use your maiden name. Does that mean you haven't married again?" Trent said.

"No, I…no, I haven't remarried."

"You should have married again, Kate, and had other children."

"It's not too late," she told him. "I still could. But what about you? I halfway expected to find you married and…" She cleared her throat. "I heard you were the man about town and it was the lady voters who got you elected to the judgeship."

Trent chuckled. "You listened to local gossip while you were in town."

"Only to Mr. Walding, the clerk at the Magnolia House."

"Did he mention my dating a lady named Molly Stoddard?"

Tension tightened Kate's muscles. "No, he didn't."

"Molly is a widow with two children. We've been

dating for about a year. Steadily these past three months."

"Then it's a serious relationship?" Kate asked, although she already knew it was; otherwise he'd have never mentioned the woman.

"It's been heading that way." Trent gripped the steering wheel with white-knuckled strength. "What about you? Anyone special in your life?"

"Hmm." *No, there's no one special, but I wish there was.* She didn't want him to think she'd been pining away for him all these years. "As a matter of fact, I've been seeing a great deal of another Dundee agent. We're very close" *Damn, Kate, that's it—just lie to the man.* But she wasn't really lying. She and Lucie Evans did see a great deal of each other. They were close—the best of friends. Girlfriends, that is. There was nothing romantic in their relationship.

"I'm glad you have someone. Are you and—what did you say his name was?"

"His name? Uh, er, Evans. Lu-Luke Evans." *Now you've really lied and you can't deny it,* she told herself. *There is no Luke Evans!*

"Are you and Luke planning on getting married?"

"No, marriage isn't in our immediate plans." That much was true—neither she nor Lucie had any wedding plans. As a matter of fact neither of them were even dating anybody seriously.

"I've been thinking about asking Molly to marry me."

"What?" She hadn't meant to react by practically screaming her response, but his statement had surprised her. No, it had more than surprised her. It had struck a nerve. Even after being divorced for over ten years, she supposed she still thought of Trent as her husband. "I'm happy for you and...I wish you the very best."

"I haven't asked her, yet. I've just been thinking about it. But I'm not getting any younger. I'm going on forty. And Molly's a wonderful person and I adore her kids."

Molly was wonderful. He adored her kids. Was that any reason to marry a person? Once she wouldn't have thought so. Now, she wasn't sure. Maybe the second time around, a person should look for something other than mad, passionate love. Maybe that's what she should do. Find a wonderful man and settle for contentment instead of passion.

Get real, Kate, you'd never settle for anything less than being in love and you know it.

"Did you tell Molly that you were leaving town with your ex-wife?" Kate asked.

"Yes, of course. I phoned her last night and explained the situation. She was very understanding. That's the way Molly is. Understanding and kind and—"

"Do you love her?" Oh, God, why had she asked him that?

Silence.

"Okay, don't answer," Kate said. "It's none of my business. Sorry I asked."

A long silence followed, then minutes later, Trent spoke. "Do you love Luke?"

"Ah…yes, I do." At least that wasn't a lie. Not entirely. Since there was no Luke, her reply was a half-lie. She did love Lucie, like a sister. That was the truth.

Trent chuckled nervously. "How did we ever get on the subject of love? It's an odd topic for us to be discussing, all things considered."

"I'll choose a safer topic," she said. "How is Aunt—Miss Mary Belle doing since she had a stroke last year?"

"Better than anyone, including the doctors, predicted she would. She's a stubborn, determined woman. Luckily, her mind wasn't affected, just her body. She couldn't walk or use her left arm for days afterward, but with intense physical therapy she came around. She worked like the devil, pushed herself hard to recover."

"She looked well."

"You noticed the cane, of course. That's probably permanent."

"She seemed very much the same and yet different somehow. The minute she entered my hotel room, she corrected me because I'd been less than mannerly when I invited her in."

Trent grinned. "That's just who she is, and who she was raised to be. You never understood that for Aunt Mary Belle there is nothing more important than good manners."

"Oh, I understood all right. Good manners was— is—a religion to her."

"You said you noticed a change in Aunt Mary Belle." As Trent turned north on US Highway 82, he hazarded a quick glance at Kate. "What sort of change?"

"I don't know exactly. It was just that she said something odd."

"What did she say?"

"She said she was capable of admitting when she was wrong and that she'd been wrong about me."

Trent glanced at Kate and smiled. "She said that, did she?"

"Yes, she did. What did she mean?"

"Why didn't you ask her?"

"I think I was too stunned to hear Mary Belle Winston admit she could be wrong about anything."

"She was never as bad as you thought she was,"

Trent said, and before Kate could respond, he added,
"And never as blameless as I thought she was."

Kate sat there quietly, absorbing Trent's words, letting them play over in her mind. He was right. Mary
Belle wasn't the monster Kate had thought her to be. If
only Trent had been able to realize, years ago, how his
aunt had manipulated him, how she'd made Kate feel
unworthy of being his wife. Hindsight is, as they say,
twenty-twenty. For everyone. For her. For Trent. And
maybe for Aunt Mary Belle, too.

"I suppose there's more than enough blame to go
around, isn't there?" Instinctively Kate reached out to
touch Trent's arm in a gesture of comfort, but stopped
when she realized what she'd been about to do. Physical contact between them was a bad idea. She had to
keep things cordial, but not too friendly. She and Trent
could never be just friends, even if they both wanted it
that way. They could be Mary Kate's parents. Nothing
more.

"What happened to Mary Kate wasn't your fault,"
Trent said.

"I know that now." But it would have been nice to
have heard her husband tell her that right after their
child was taken from them. Instead, every time he had
looked at her in the days and weeks following their baby's abduction, there had been accusation in his eyes.
And when Aunt Mary Belle had come right out and
said, "If only you hadn't stormed off on your own the
way you did, this wouldn't have happened," Trent had
remained silent, hadn't uttered one word in his wife's
defense.

A heavy silence hung between them. Kate assumed
Trent was lost in the past, as she was, reliving painful
memories.

Nearly an hour later, Trent broke the silence. "Do you want to stop for an early lunch in Birmingham or would your rather stop somewhere between Birmingham and Tupelo?"

"It doesn't matter," she replied. "I could wait until we get to Memphis. I ate a big breakfast."

He wondered how many times Kate missed meals. She looked a little underweight to him, but not as thin and unhealthy as she'd looked the last time he saw her. After their daughter's kidnapping, Kate had stopped eating, stopped sleeping, stopped living.

"We'll stop and get a bite along the way," he said. "Maybe we'll run across an old-fashioned burger joint somewhere. Do you still love greasy cheeseburgers with the works?" He remembered how on their first date, she had attacked a huge cheeseburger—with onions—and eaten every bite. She was the first girl he'd dated who wasn't on a diet. He'd liked that about her—that she had a passion for life.

"Oh, yes, I still love cheeseburgers smothered in onions." She smiled at him. "Some things don't change."

Her thousand-watt smile had always turned him inside out—that sure hadn't changed. The basic male animal in him wanted to pull the Bentley off to the side of the road, undo their seat belts and drag Kate into his arms. The powerful physical attraction that had overwhelmed them when they first met, when he'd helped a damsel in distress, was still as potent as ever. He wanted her now, as he'd wanted her then; but he didn't dare act on instinct. He had no rights where Kate was concerned. He'd let her go over ten years ago and now she had a new life and a new love.

Why did that bother him so damn much? It wasn't as if he was still in love with her. And it wasn't as if he didn't have someone special in his life. But he wasn't in love with Molly, either. Being in love was highly overrated, wasn't it? He could have a good life with Molly and he could be a loving and caring stepfather to her children. After all, it wasn't as if he could turn back the clock and make things right with Kate again.

If you could, would you? that damn irritating inner voice asked. It was a moot question.

He could no more have Kate back than the infant Mary Kate could be returned to them.

"Kate?"

"Hmm?"

"Have you actually thought all this through?" he asked. "I mean do you know how you'll deal with whatever we find out, be it good news or bad?"

"I'll deal with the news—good or bad—the way I have for the past eleven and a half years. If none of the little girls turn out to be Mary Kate, I'll keep on searching." She paused briefly. "For the rest of my life."

"Is that what you've been doing all these years, searching for our little girl?"

She nodded. "Except for money to pay for life's necessities, I've spent every penny I've made searching for Mary Kate. One of the reasons I left the Atlanta police department and joined Dundee's is because I knew as one of their agents I would get a discount on services and I'd have all their vast resources at my disposal."

"What if one of these little girls is Mary Kate? What will you do then?"

Crossing her arms at the waist and gripping her elbows, Kate hugged herself as if she'd had a sudden chill. "If we find our daughter, I want to see her. And I want to know all about her life. Who her parents are. If she has brothers and sisters. Is she healthy and happy."

"And if she is happy and healthy and part of a loving family, then what?"

Kate clenched her jaw and shut her eyes. Trent caught a glimpse of the pain on her face, but looked away quickly, unable to bear seeing her suffer. But this time, whatever the outcome, he intended to stand by her and help her deal with the fallout.

"I'd like to believe I'll be able to walk away and not disrupt her life," Kate said. "But I don't know if I'm that strong."

"You are," he told her. "We have to be. Both of us."

"It'll have to be enough, won't it? To see her. Once. And then go away and leave her to her happy life with people she thinks of as her parents."

"You should have another child," Trent said. "You were born to be a mother."

"No other child could ever replace Mary Kate."

"I know that only too well. I don't think I ever want to father another child," he admitted, surprised that he'd actually said the words aloud. He'd never told another living soul that he was afraid to love another child as he had loved Mary Kate, that the fear of losing another child was too great.

Kate turned sideways in her seat and stared at him. "I feel the same way. I can't bear the thought of ever again going through the hell we went through when we lost Mary Kate. I'm afraid to have another baby, so you see I understand the way you feel, only too well."

He glanced at her hurriedly, then just as he looked back at the long stretch of Interstate 65 ahead of them, Kate touched his arm. A tender, caressing squeeze that sent shock waves through his entire body.

Oh, God, why had she touched him?

Trent gritted his teeth in an effort to ward off the

emotional demons that plagued him whenever he thought about all that he'd lost. First his daughter. And then his wife. But his wife—his ex-wife—had come back into his life and she was leading him into the unknown, into dangerous waters. It had taken him ten years to put his life back together and to begin thinking about a future with another woman. And damn it all, here he was heading toward Memphis with Kate—the love of his life—on a journey that might well lead them straight to a hell even more horrible than the one they'd barely survived eleven years ago.

Four

Kate didn't put up a fuss when Trent drove straight into downtown Memphis to the Peabody Hotel. She could have told him it would have been nice if he'd asked her where she wanted to stay, but what was the point? After all, he hadn't considered paying for a two-bedroom suite at a prestigious Memphis landmark hotel as anything out of the ordinary. Having been born with the proverbial silver spoon in his mouth, Trent always traveled first class.

"I phoned last night to make reservations," he'd told her when they came through Germantown on the outskirts of the city. "I booked the two-bedroom suite for a week, with the understanding I might need it longer."

Kate had nodded and smiled as if she were accustomed to having someone else make her decisions for her. But why should she complain? Staying at the most elegant hotel in town sure beat staying at a fifty-dollara-night motel, which was what she could afford on her budget.

Her bedroom was luxurious, as was her bath. And the large bed looked inviting. The bellman placed her bag on the suitcase rack and returned to the sitting room. She watched as Trent tipped the man. From the smile on the bellman's face, she figured it was more money than most people gave him.

"Would you like to have supper at *Chez Philippe* or the *Capriccio* Restaurant here at the hotel? Of if you prefer, we can go out to a nearby restaurant." Trent removed his overcoat and tossed it across a nearby chair in the lounge. "Our other choice is to eat in. I could order room service."

She debated her possible replies. She really didn't want to go out, but would eating dinner alone with Trent in their suite be too intimate?

"I'm tired. I'd rather eat in and get to bed early," she told him. "So, if you'd order for me, anything will do. I'm not particular. Just no regular coffee this late in the day. While you do that, I'll use my cell phone to contact Special Agent Moran."

"Steak, pork, chicken or seafood?" Trent called out as he sat down at the desk and picked up the room service menu.

"I'm not really all that hungry," she told him. "Not after the burgers we ate in Tupelo. A salad would do fine for me."

Kate shrugged off her coat, then hung it in the closet. She wasn't exactly a neat-freak, but she had an orderly mind and liked everything in its place. She'd been that way all her life. It had been one of the few things about her that Aunt Mary Belle had approved of during her brief marriage to Trent. Kate removed her scarf and gloves, placed them on the shelf at the top of the closet, and then kicked off her shoes and lined them side-by-side in the closet floor.

When she walked to the door, she heard Trent on the phone, ordering their dinner. After studying him closely, she closed the door and tried to blot out his image. Now was the time to take control of any lingering sexual feelings she had for her ex-husband. They were going to be together for days, perhaps weeks, and she couldn't go around mooning over a guy who was practically engaged to another woman. No matter what happened with the search for Mary Kate, there was no future for Trent and her. Her mind understood; her heart didn't. And she wasn't even going to think about how her libido reacted every time Trent came near her.

After sitting down on the edge of the bed, she removed her cell phone from her purse and hit the button that instantly dialed Dante Moran's number. As she waited while the phone rang, she wriggled her sock-covered toes. On the job for Dundee's she wore slacks all the time and preferred socks to knee-highs. It had been ages since she's put on a dress. Actually she owned two dresses and one suit. Everything else in her closet was slacks, tops and jackets. She almost wished she had brought along one of her two dresses, just in case she needed it.

She shouldn't do this to herself—shouldn't think about pleasing Trent. He'd always preferred her in dresses, telling her numerous times that it was a shame to cover up a great pair of legs.

"Special Agent Moran," the deep male voice said.

"Yes, Moran, it's Kate Malone."

"Are you still in Prospect?"

"No, I'm back in Memphis. Trent came with me. We're at the Peabody. In a suite. A two-bedroom suite."

Moran whistled. "Putting on the Ritz, huh? But I guess your ex-hubby can afford it, can't he?"

"Oh, yes, he can easily afford it." Kate nervously bounced her knees up and down until she realized what she was doing, then stopped abruptly. "So, what's the latest? Has there been any word on—"

"We've found three sets of other parents who lost infant daughters around the same time Mary Kate was taken. Similar circumstances. All the babies were blond and under six months old. We've contacted these people and if everybody makes it to Memphis by eleven o'clock tomorrow, we'll have a general meeting to go over the situation."

"Did you say three sets of parents?" she asked. "But…there are only three little girls. That means—"

"It means we've got four sets of biological parents and only three children who might belong to them."

Kate swallowed hard. She didn't wish heartbreak for anyone else, but she couldn't help praying that Mary Kate was one of those three little girls. "What do you know about these people?"

"All I can tell you is that out of those three sets, only one couple is still married. They're eager to find out if one of the little girls is theirs. They have two other children now. One couple is divorced, like you and Trent, and both of them are interested in finding out if one of the children is theirs. And then there's a father whose wife died three years ago. He's hoping one child is his."

"Is the method of positive ID still going to be DNA tests?" Kate asked. Moran had said that although they could match up blood types and infant footprints, the most reliable testing was DNA. Each little girl's DNA would be compared to the possible birth parents.

"Yeah. And we will speed up that process. Your boss

man, MacNamara, has called in some favors, as has
Sam Dundee, to get a rush job for you."

Thank you, Sawyer MacNamara, Kate said silently.
Although her best friend and fellow Dundee agent,
Lucie Evans, absolutely despised the CEO of Dundee's,
Kate had always liked the man. Now she positively
loved him. But she wouldn't tell Lucie. Kate smiled to
herself.

Sam Dundee was a man everyone liked and admired.
Being a father himself, he no doubt understood how important this was to her. Once this was all over, she'd
have to phone both Sawyer and Mr. Dundee to thank
them.

"Have the adoptive parents been notified?" she
asked.

"That process has already begun. And we're starting
with the older children first, so since Mary Kate would
be nearly twelve years old now, she'll be in the first set."

Kate's chest tightened. *Please, dear God, please, let
her be one of these little girls.*

"How soon do you think—?" Kate breathed deeply,
then sighed. "How long before we give samples for the
DNA tests?"

"Hopefully we'll take samples tomorrow. And within
a couple of days, we should be able to set up a meeting
with the adoptive parents." Moran paused. "We're asking each of the adoptive parents to bring pictures of their
child."

"You'd think a mother would be able to know her
own child from a photograph, wouldn't you?" Fear and
uncertainty welled up inside Kate. What if she looked
at those pictures and didn't recognize Mary Kate?
"What if—" her voice cracked. "I may not know my
own daughter."

Tears stung her eyes. Dammit, she didn't cry. Not anymore. She'd shed all her tears years ago. Or at least she thought she had.

"Look, Kate, don't do this to yourself," Moran said. "Once we get the DNA results, you'll know for sure."

"Yes, you're right. Sorry about getting all female and emotional on you. I know how you G-men hate emotion." She forced a laugh.

"Lady, if anyone is entitled to get a little emotional about this, you are. If I were in your shoes, I'd be emotional."

Kate really laughed then. "You're kidding me, right? Dante Moran is a man of steel."

He chuckled. "Yeah, I do have that reputation, don't I? But truth be told, we're all emotional when it comes to personal things, even if we don't outwardly show that emotion."

"You know what, Special Agent Moran? I think I like you."

"And you know what, Kate Malone? I know I like you."

"Friends?" she asked.

"Yeah," he said. "I'll call you in the morning if the meeting at eleven o'clock is a go."

"Okay. Thanks."

Kate hit the Off button and laid her phone on the nightstand, then spread out across the bed and tried to relax. If things were different, she just might pursue a personal relationship with Moran. From certain things he'd said, she figured he had some romantic tragedy in his past and that's why he was still single. Most of the good ones were taken by the time they were thirty-five. And Moran had told her himself that he'd never been married.

Oh, we'd make a fine pair, both of us still halfway in love with other people. Dante with the mystery lady from his past, she with Trent. Yes, she was still partly hung up on Trent. She probably always would be. When you loved someone the way she'd loved Trent, it never completely went away. A part of her would always love him.

A soft knock sounded on the door. She sat straight up in the middle of the bed.

"Yes?"

"Dinner will be here in about thirty-five minutes," Trent said through the closed door.

"Fine. Thanks. That'll give me time for a quick nap."

"I'll let you know when dinner arrives."

"Okay."

"Kate, are you all right? Is something wrong?"

Go away, she thought. *Yes, something's wrong. I'm still hung up on you and there doesn't seem to be anything I can do about it.*

"I talked to Moran," Kate said.

"May I come in?" Trent asked.

Oh, great. Just great. "I…uh…okay, sure." She scooted to the edge of the bed and was halfway standing when Trent opened the door.

He looked at her. She looked at him. He frowned.

"Have you been crying?" He came toward her slowly, as if uncertain whether he should.

"No. I don't cry. Not anymore."

He paused when he was within a couple of feet of her. "What did Moran say to upset you?"

"I'm not upset."

"Okay, so what is it? Something's bothering you. I know how you are when—"

"No, Trent, you do not know me," she practically

screamed at him. "You don't have the slightest idea who I am. I'm not sure you ever did."

His shoulders slumped. His frown deepened. "That's not fair, Kate. You could be right about my not knowing the person you are now, but I did know you once. And you knew me. We knew each other inside out." He moved closer, reached out and lifted her hand, then placed it over his heart. "There was a time when I thought—" He dropped his hold on her as if her hand had suddenly become red-hot. "Sorry. Old habits die hard, I guess. Being with you brings back a lot of memories. Good memories."

Don't look back, she told herself. *Don't get sucked in by all those good memories.* She needed to take charge of this situation. Set a precedent here and now. Their past relationship was off-limits. It was in the past and should stay there.

"Moran will call tomorrow if a meeting he's trying to set up works out," Kate said, deliberately changing the subject. "They've found three other sets of people who may be the parents of those three little girls. With us that makes four, so one set of parents is going to be disappointed after the DNA tests results come back."

"You're afraid we'll be those parents, aren't you? That's what's wrong." He gazed at her, kindness and concern in his dark eyes. And true understanding. "You have to know how much I want one of those little girls to be Mary Kate. I want it as much as you do."

She knew he was telling her the truth. As Mary Kate's father, he wanted what Kate wanted. But she also knew that he hadn't dreamed of the day, hoped and prayed for the day, lived for the day that Mary Kate would be found. But she had. Not one single day had passed in the eleven years and nine months since their child had been stolen from them that Kate hadn't longed for the moment she would see her daughter again. No, Trent had chosen a different path—he had believed Mary Kate was dead, that she was lost to them forever.

"I'd like to be alone for a while," she told him, her voice deadly calm. "Please, let me know when dinner is ready."

With a hurt expression on his face, he turned around and walked out of her bedroom. When he closed the door, Kate rushed into the bathroom, turned on the faucets and gathered water in her hands. After splashing her face with cool water several times, she dried her face and hands, then clenched her teeth together tightly, trying her best not to cry.

Things weren't going to get any better between Trent and her. Not only did the past stand between them, a painful reminder of how much they had lost, but the sexual tension smoldering just below the surface frightened her. It would be so easy to fall into Trent's arm, to fall into his bed, in an effort to recapture what they'd once shared. No matter what happened, even if one of those three little girls turned out to be their daughter, Mary Kate would never be her child again. And even if she succumbed to her feelings for Trent, they couldn't go back. It was too late for them. Too late for all of them.

Trent poured himself another cup of decaf coffee, then relaxed across the table from Kate where they'd shared a delicious meal in the suite's spacious lounge. They'd also shared some mundane conversation while they dined—Kate on her Caesar salad and he on his salmon fillet.

"I ordered dessert." With his free hand, Trent lifted the silver lid covering the plate containing a huge chocolate brownie smothered in whipped cream and pecans. "I hope brownies are still your favorite dessert. Brownies aren't a specialty of either hotel restaurant, but they aim to please their guests, so they actually sent out to a bakery."

"My food preferences haven't changed much," she admitted. "At lunch you remembered about the cheeseburgers and tonight you went to a great deal of trouble to see that I got my all-time favorite dessert. You're being very nice to me. And I'm afraid I haven't been all that nice to you. I'm sorry. It's just—"

"You've been nice enough," Trent said. "Besides, why should you be nice to me? I wasn't exactly the ideal husband at a time when you needed me most. I was too wrapped up in my own grief and guilt to help you."

She stared at him, her expression telling him that she was uncertain she'd heard him correctly. "Was that some sort of apology?"

"If an apology will do you any good now, then I'll apologize until I'm blue in the face. I'm sorry, Kate." He set the cup and saucer on the table, shoved back his chair and stood. "God, how you must have hated me." He walked across the room to the windows and looked out over downtown Memphis. Dressed in brilliant lights more sparkling than diamonds, the River City came alive at night, like a beautiful woman decked out in all her finery. A part of him wished he could walk out into the night and disappear. He'd managed to keep his demons at bay for so many years, pretending he didn't care, telling himself over and over again that Mary Kate was dead and that he'd never see either his daughter or his wife ever again. But reality had made a lie of all the beliefs he'd clung to for the past eleven years, ever since Kate had walked out on him. Now Kate was back in his life, even if for only a few weeks. And if fate was on their side, they'd see their daughter soon.

Damn, why hadn't he listened to Kate all those years ago when she'd insisted she was going to find their baby? He should have helped her hunt for Mary Kate. Instead, he'd crawled into a dark, emotionally barren hole and cut himself off from hope and from love.

He felt her presence directly behind him, even before she laid her hand on his shoulder. The minute she touched him, he tensed. God, how he wanted to hold her. Hold her and never let her go.

"Trent?"

He clenched his jaw.

"It's all right," she told him.

"No, it's not all right. I failed you. And I'm sorry about that."

"Neither of us was equipped to handle losing our baby. We each dealt with it the best we could. But what hurt me the most was your agreeing with Aunt Mary Belle that it was all my fault."

What had she said? Trent snapped around and glared at Kate. "Aunt Mary Belle never said it was all your fault. God, Kate, she never—"

"She said that if I hadn't run off angry that Sunday after church and taken Mary Kate with me, none of it would have happened. Don't you dare deny that she said it."

"Yes, she did say that, but she also said that if only she had agreed to walk with us, the way she should have, it wouldn't have happened. Don't you remember her saying—?"

"You're lying!"

"No, you don't remember, do you? By the time Aunt Mary Belle told me she blamed herself, you'd already run out of the room."

Kate stared at him in disbelief.

"Are you telling me that all these years you've thought I blamed you for what happened?" he asked.

"You did blame me. You and Aunt Mary Belle both blamed me."

He stared at her, hurt and anger mixing with love and understanding inside him. "Kate, honey, no one blamed you but you. You were so consumed with guilt that nobody could get through to you, not even the doctors."

When he reached out to touch her, she backed away from him.

"I can't deal with this right now," she told him. "I don't know if I believe you or not."

"Why would I lie to you? What would I have to gain?"

"I don't know, but…if you didn't blame me for what happened, then what were you apologizing for a few minutes ago?"

"For everything," he told her. "For letting what happened, happen. For not being able to make things right. For not taking better care of you. For not being able to give you what you needed to see you through the rough times. God, Kate, if I hadn't made so many mistakes, you wouldn't have left me. I failed you miserably."

"All these years, I thought I'd failed you."

Before he could pull her into his arms the way he wanted to do, she turned and fled. He hurried after her, but halted when she slammed the door in his face. He stood there for several minutes staring at the door, trying to decide if he should storm into her bedroom or leave her alone. When he heard the click of the door lock, the question was answered for him. Kate didn't want or need him. Not anymore.

Five

Kate and Trent had been the first to arrive, but within thirty minutes, everyone was assembled at the local FBI headquarters in Memphis. Dante Moran, looking every inch the federal agent in his black suit, pale gray shirt and striped tie, surveyed the group before his dark gaze settled on Kate. She offered him a hesitant smile. He understood, as she did, that when all was said and done, at least one set out of the four groups of parents here today would be gravely disappointed. There were only three adopted girls who had been stolen around Easter twelve years ago by the infant abduction ring, only three babies taken at that time who could possibly belong to them.

Avoiding eye-contact with Trent, Kate scanned the room. At breakfast earlier this morning, neither she nor Trent had brought up anything about the night before, about the blame-game that Kate didn't understand. She had truly believed that both Trent and his aunt held her responsible for Mary Kate's kidnapping. Was it possible she'd been wrong? After some major soul searching during the night, she still didn't know for sure if Trent had told her the truth. But why would he lie?

How could you have been so wrong all these years? she asked herself. *You were so sure he blamed you for Mary Kate's abduction.*

As Kate glanced from person to person, she noted a similar expression on each parent's face—that odd mixture of hope and fear. No doubt her features conveyed those same emotions. Jayne and Clay Perkins were the only couple still married. They were in their late thirties, he tall and thin, she short and plump. They had a ten-year-old son and a seven-year-old daughter. Their eldest child, Megan, who'd be almost twelve now, had been snatched from her stroller in a downtown Birmingham department store when she was three months old. A week before Easter.

Exotically dark and beautiful Jessica Previn and blond and equally attractive Dave Blankenship were divorced. His second wife, Mindy, accompanied him today, as did Jessica's fiancé, Cory. Dave had a three-year-old son by Mindy and he'd proudly shown-off his child's photos to the other parents. Jessica and Dave's daughter, Charity, had been stolen from her infant swing in the couple's Prattville backyard the day after Easter, nearly twelve years ago.

Muscularly built and sporting a military short haircut, Dennis Copeland, a widower for two years, had been left alone to raise his younger daughter, seven-year-old Brooke. His wife Stacy and he had been students at Auburn University when their first child was born. Two-month-old Heather Copeland had been abducted by a friendly stranger who'd sweet-talked the babysitter into letting her hold the child. The Copeland's babysitter had taken Heather for a stroller ride in a small park near her parents' apartment on the Thursday before Easter.

Kate couldn't help wondering how the loss of their child had affected each couple. The horrific event had no doubt proven as devastating to each of them as it had to Trent and her. Had the Blankenships' marriage disintegrated the same way her marriage had? Had they blamed each other? Or had they simply fallen out of love? What about the other two couples? How had the Perkinses and the Copelands managed to stay together? *What did it matter?* she asked herself. Although the others shared the same tragedy, they were all individuals who had their own unique relationships that had either stayed intact or had fallen apart for reasons only the two people involved knew. And maybe even they didn't know. There were times when she questioned her reasons for leaving Trent. But there was one thing everyone here today shared—a desire to know the truth about their lost child. Apparently the others were as anxious as Trent and she to find out if their daughter was still alive, if by some miracle one of these stolen baby girls might be theirs.

As Dante Moran explained in detail what the FBI knew about the infant abduction ring that had operated in the deep south for the past dozen years, Trent reached over and grasped Kate's hand. Instinctively she started to jerk away, not wanting comfort from anyone, least of all her ex-husband. She hadn't been able to trust another person completely, had chosen to go it alone, to take care of herself and not lean on any man. But common sense stopped her from rejecting Trent's touch.

Common sense and admitting to herself that an emotional bond still existed between them. After years of being apart, of now having very little in common, they still shared one of the most important links any two people can share. A child. And in their case, a missing child.

Kate found herself clasping Trent's hand tightly and inching ever so slightly toward him. She glanced at him and saw her own thoughts and feelings reflected in his eyes. He leaned over and said quietly, "Meeting these other parents makes me wish the FBI had found four little girls."

Kate nodded. "Someone's daughter is still missing, her fate unknown." She gulped down her fear. "Mary Kate may not be one of the these children. We could be the parents whose hearts are broken all over again."

Trent slipped his arm around Kate's shoulders. Understanding his intention, she realized she welcomed the comfort he offered. Truth be told, she was glad she wasn't facing this traumatic experience alone. None of this would be easy whether or not they found Mary Kate.

"The bureau is in the process of notifying all the adoptive parents. They number in the hundreds. We have begun with the oldest children. The three baby girls we believe were taken from within a two-hundred-mile radius in Alabama on or around Easter Sunday twelve years ago this coming April are among the first to be processed. We're asking the adoptive parents of these three young girls to cooperate by allowing us to take DNA samples of their adopted child," Moran said. "Here today we'll try to answer any questions y'all have. Then we want the birth parents to give us DNA samples. These tests will take top priority. One of the birth parents has agreed to pay the expenses to have these four tests done by an independent lab to expedite the matter, so we should know something in a week or less. The DNA tests will confirm paternity. We'll also use blood types and any footprints or fingerprints available for each child."

Kate turned to Trent. "Did you—?"

"Yes."

"Thank you."

"I offered to cover the cost of the DNA tests so we wouldn't have to wait any longer than absolutely necessary," he said softly, for her ears only. "I'd pay ten times that much to find out the truth for us…and for these other parents." He inclined his head toward the others.

"Even if these girls belong to any three couples here, that doesn't mean you'll be able to walk in and claim your child," Moran explained. "We're dealing with a legal nightmare. The adoptive parents of these three girls are already hiring lawyers, as I'm sure will countless hundreds of other adoptive parents in the weeks and months ahead."

"What rights do we have?" Dennis Copeland asked.

"That's probably going to be a decision the courts have to make."

"Are all these girls in good homes?" Jessica Previn asked. "Do they all have loving parents?"

"I don't have that kind of detailed information at this time," Moran told her.

"When do we get to meet the adoptive parents?" Jayne Perkins asked.

"Will we be shown pictures of the girls?" Jessica Previn questioned. "I'm sure I could pick out Charity if I saw her."

"I agree," Jayne said. "I feel certain I'd know Megan the minute I laid eyes on her."

"We plan to try to set up a meeting with the adoptive parents of these three girls, hopefully very soon, within a day or two," Moran said. "We'll ask each to bring pictures of their child. But I caution y'all not to get your hopes up, even if you see photographs of these girls. Your infant daughters were all blond. Two were blue-eyed and two brown-eyed. As we all know hair and eye colors can change over the years. Blondes can become brunettes. And blue eyes can turn green or even brown. And it's been known for children with chocolate brown eyes as babies to have hazel eyes as teenagers."

"Should we birth parents hire our own lawyers?" Dave Blankenship asked.

"I can't advise you on that," Moran replied.

"If you were one of us, what would you do?" Trent asked, then answered his own question, "You'd hire a lawyer, wouldn't you?" Trent looked from parent to parent as he spoke. "I've already contacted my lawyer about this matter and I'd recommend that y'all do the same. I'm sure all of you, like Kate and I, want only what's best for your child—if it turns out one of these girls is your child. What's best may well mean leaving our daughters with their adoptive parents, but even in that case, we'll still want our rights, as the biological parents, protected."

A loud murmur rose from the other parents as they discussed their options amongst themselves. To a person, they all agreed that each couple would hire a lawyer of their own.

"I'll be in touch with y'all when I receive any more pertinent information," Moran told them. "And as soon as we can work something out for a meeting with the adoptive parents, we'll let you know. In the meantime, a technician from O'Steen Labs is here to take your DNA samples. Special Agent Clark will escort y'all, couple by couple, into his office where the technician is waiting. And I want to assure everyone that these DNA samples will be properly collected and will be under FBI protection from here to the lab, as will the results."

As the other couples exited the room, Moran motioned to Kate. Leaving Trent standing by the door, she made her way to the FBI agent.

"Do you know your blood type and your hus—your ex-husband's?" Moran asked.

Kate's heart fluttered with anticipation. "Yes, I know. Why do you ask?"

"What are the blood types?"

"Mine is A-positive and Trent's is O-positive."

"Two of the three girls have O-positive blood type."

Kate swallowed hard. Warmth flushed her face and neck. "Mary Kate has O-positive, the same as Trent."

Moran glanced at Trent, then back at Kate. "I thought you should know. But don't get your hopes up. More people have O-positive than any other blood type. Could be one out of each set of parents has type O."

"I realize that. But at least, it puts us in the running, doesn't it?"

Moran gave her a tender look, one that told her he sympathized. But he didn't touch her or say anything else before he turned and walked away. Strange man, she thought. A mixture of toughness and kindness.

"What was that all about?" Trent approached Kate. "From the way he was looking at you, I'd say Special Agent Moran has a personal interest in you."

"Dante Moran and I are colleagues of a sort. And oddly enough, I think we understand each other. But there is nothing romantic between us." Why had she felt compelled to explain her relationship with Moran to Trent?

"If Luke wasn't in the picture, things might be different, right?"

Oh, God, she'd forgotten about that stupid lie—the one about Luke being the man in her life. There was no Luke. Only Lucie, her best friend. "Look, Trent, I think you should know that Luke is—"

Kate's cell phone rang. Saved by the bell? she wondered.

She flipped open the phone and said, "Malone here."

"Kate, it's Lucie. How are you? What's going on? Where are you?"

"Speak of the devil." Kate chuckled. "Now, how about slowing down. You're shooting questions at me ninety-to-nothing."

"Sorry. It's just that I haven't heard from you in a couple of days, not since you were headed out to Prospect to talk to your ex."

"Trent and I are in Memphis, at FBI headquarters. We just sat in on a general meeting with three other pairs of biological parents. Everyone is submitting samples for DNA testing and the Feds should be able to match up the three girls to their biological parents within a week. Dante Moran is doing his best to help me, although his hands are somewhat tied by the system."

"From all I hear, Moran's a good guy, if a bit unfriendly," Lucie said. "And considering the fact that he supposedly has some difficulty with rules and regulations, I figure it's only a matter of time before he jumps ship and joins Dundee's."

"You're kidding? Is there word around the office about—"

"Daisy let it slip that our fearless leader has made the offer to Moran, and you know Sawyer wouldn't do that unless he was damn sure Moran is interested."

"Moran hasn't said a word to me about it."

"Why should he?" Lucie laughed. "Don't tell me that you and Moran are—"

"No, we are not. We like and respect each other, but that's all there is to it." Kate eyed Trent, who was listening quite intensely to her end of the conversation.

"Okay. So how's the chemistry between you and your ex? You've still got feelings for him and don't deny it. I'm your best buddy and I know you. Does he still have a thing for you?"

"Can't say."

"Is he with you right now?"

"Yes."

"Mmm, hmm. So, call me later with details, okay? I just got back to Atlanta last night and I've told Sawyer that I need a little downtime before he sends me out again. The man's being a real ass about my assignments lately. Ever since our last big brouhaha, he's been putting me on wuss jobs because he knows how I hate being put on lightweight assignments simply because I'm a woman. I swear, Kate, one of these days I'm going to cut that guy down to size."

Kate laughed. "If anybody can do it, you can. But be prepared for a battle royal. We both know that nothing would please Sawyer more than for you to give him a legitimate reason to fire you. You're the thorn in his side, honey, and the only reason you're still with Dundee's is because Sawyer has worked hard to not let his personal feelings dictate his business decisions."

"Let's face facts—neither Sawyer nor I can be impersonal about anything that goes on between us. We can't stand each other and nothing will change that fact." Lucie groaned. "Would you listen to me belly-aching about my stupid feud with the black knight when you've got a major deal going on in your life right now."

Kate's gaze met Trent's and she realized he was curious about her caller. Was now the time to come clean and tell him that Luke was really Lucie? Should she or shouldn't she be honest with him? Having a boyfriend, albeit a fictional one, provided her with a barrier between Trent and her. If she removed that obstacle, would Trent make a move on her or would he remain true to his lady friend, Molly? The God's honest truth was that Kate still had it bad for her ex and it wouldn't take much for her to fall into his arms—or into his bed, for that matter.

"I need a favor," Kate said.

"You name it, you got it."

"I need you to go over to my apartment and water my plants."

"You do, do you?"

Kate didn't have any houseplants and Lucie knew it. The catch phrase she'd just repeated had been a code that Lucie used whenever she found herself in a situation with a guy that she couldn't handle. If Lucie was in danger of giving in to lust and knew she'd regret it in the morning, she'd call Kate with a spiel about watering her plants, which was actually a cry for immediate help. Lucie had a notorious black thumb. She could kill any plant within ten days without even trying.

"It could be a week or two before I get back to Atlanta and I wouldn't want anything to happen to my plants," Kate said.

"Want me to come to Memphis or just be available in case things get dicey?"

"The latter."

"I'll be available." Pause. "Kate, I hope one of those kids turns out to be Mary Kate."

"Yeah, me, too."

"Take care, huh."

"You, too."

Kate closed her phone and returned it to her jacket pocket.

Trent clutched her shoulder. "Was that Luke?"

"Yes and no," Kate admitted.

Trent stared at her, a puzzled expression on his face.

"I was talking to my best friend, Lucie Evans, who is a former FBI agent and now a fellow Dundee employee." Kate sighed loudly. "There is no Luke. Just Lucie. I do love her. She's practically like a sister to me. So I only partly lied to you."

Trent grinned. "Why did you lie about having a boyfriend?"

"Want me to be totally honest?"

He nodded.

"I still have feelings for you and I sense you have some for me, too. It's probably just some leftover lust, but… I thought having a boyfriend might keep you at arm's length."

Trent eased his hand down her shoulder and circled her waist. Looking her square in the eyes, he told her, "If I wanted you and you wanted me, too, a hundred boyfriends wouldn't stop me from making love to you."

Excitement shot through Kate like Fourth of July fireworks. "Trent…I…we—"

He pulled her up against him and lowered his head. His lips came down, down, down.

"The lab technician is ready for you two," Dante Moran called from the doorway.

Kate froze. Trent lifted his head and reluctantly released her.

That was a close call, she thought. The next time it happens—and it would—what if there was nobody around to interrupt them?

Six

Kate sat across the table from Dante Moran in a back booth at the River City Café, an old-fashioned fifties diner not far from the FBI field office. After she and Trent gave the lab technician their DNA samples, she'd insisted that Trent go back to the hotel without her.

"I need to put some space between us," she'd admitted. "I think you need that, too. Why don't you go back to the Peabody and find something to do to pass the time? I want to stay here and go over any records belonging to the abduction ring that Moran will let me look at. I can't handle more than one major problem at a time and dealing with you—with all the old feelings we once had for each other—is posing a big problem for me."

Trent hadn't said much in response; he'd just agreed with her and left. A part of her had been disappointed that he hadn't put up a fight, that he hadn't proclaimed his feelings for her weren't just remnants of a past love.

"Shouldn't you call your ex-husband and let him know you're okay and won't be back to the hotel until later?" Moran glanced over the edge of the menu he held as he questioned Kate.

"I don't have to report in to Trent. We are divorced and the only reason we're together now is because of Mary Kate."

"What did the guy do to you to make you hate him?"

"I don't hate—"

The waitress came to their booth, placed glasses of water in front of them and asked, "So, what'll it be?"

"I'll take the chicken and dressing special," Moran said. "And coffee. Black."

The waitress, a gum-smacking twenty-year-old with spiked white hair, turned to Kate. "And you, ma'am?"

That "ma'am" made Kate feel old. She was only thirty-five. But a world-weary thirty-five. Looking up at the young girl, she replied, "I want the grilled chicken salad and coffee. And I'll need creamer for my coffee."

As soon as the waitress left, Moran rephrased his earlier question. "What's with you and your ex?"

"You're being awfully nosey."

Moran grinned, his teeth pearly-white against his bronze complexion. "I thought maybe you needed to talk about it. If I'm wrong, I apologize."

Kate sighed. "There's nothing to talk about. Trent and I have been divorced for ten years. He's practically engaged to someone else." She looked right at Moran. "And I do not hate Trent. That's the problem. It would be much easier if I did hate him."

"Mmm, hmm."

"Hey, I appreciate your letting me hang around the office all day. And I really have to thank you for giving me access to those files. Will you get in trouble for doing that?"

"Not unless somebody tells on me." He grinned. "To be honest, I'm not greatly concerned about my career with the bureau. I've been giving a great deal of thought to changing jobs."

"Why would you do that?" *So, Lucie's info about Moran leaving the FBI and coming to work for Dundee's was true,* Kate thought.

"My career with the bureau is at a standstill and I'm not likely to move on up, not with my reputation as a rebel."

The waitress brought their coffee and small containers of creamer for Kate. Moran lifted the mug to his lips and sipped the hot brew. After emptying two tiny cartons of creamer into her coffee, Kate stirred it until the black turned a luscious café au lait color.

"Is that a rebel with or without a cause?" she asked.

Moran chuckled. "That depends on who you ask. As far as I'm concerned, I always have a cause. Sometimes I don't play by the rules, but there's always logic behind the madness."

"Do you think this infant abduction ring case will be your last?"

"Yeah, it could be. We should wrap up my part of things within a month, then I'm thinking about moving back south."

"To Atlanta?"

Moran lifted an eyebrow inquisitively. "Who at Dundee's has been talking?"

"Our office manager, Daisy Holbrook, told my buddy Lucie and Lucie told me when we spoke earlier today." Kate smiled at Moran. "If you want my opinion…?"

"Fire away."

"I think Dundee's would be damn lucky to get a man like you."

"Why thank you, ma'am."

"I guess you already know that the pay is very good, as are the benefits. Some assignments are dangerous, some are heartbreaking, some are routine and a few are just downright boring. But Sawyer MacNamara is a top-notch boss. Smart, savvy, fair-minded. Except when it comes to Lucie Evans. With those two, it's tit for tat. Don't listen to anything Lucie says about Sawyer or vice versa. They hate each other with a passion."

"How is it that they're able to work together? Why hasn't Lucie quit or MacNamara fired her if the animosity between them is that bad?"

Kate shrugged. "Lucie would never quit and give Sawyer the satisfaction. He won't fire her because everybody would know he'd done it for personal reasons."

"What about Dundee himself? If MacNamara runs the show on a day-to-day basis, how much input does the owner have?"

"Sam Dundee comes to town at least once a year, occasionally more often if a particular case intrigues him. He's kept informed and if there's ever a conflict for Sawyer, Sam steps in. You'll like Sam. Everybody does. And you won't find a better bunch of professionals anywhere than at Dundee's."

"Tell me something, Kate Malone—are all the female agents as good-looking as you?"

"Humph." Kate couldn't help smiling. "That could be considered a chauvinist statement."

"It wasn't meant to be. Take it as it was meant—as a compliment."

"In that case, yes, all the female agents are attractive,

in their own way. Right now there are only two other female agents. The office manager is female and three of the four office staff are, too. Lucie Evans, my dear friend, is former FBI, as is Sawyer. Their feud goes back to the time they worked for the bureau and neither will talk about it. Lucie's gorgeous. Nearly six feet tall. I'd describe her as a modern-day, brown-eyed, redheaded amazon."

Moran let out a long, low whistle. "Maybe the problem between MacNamara and her is that she's too much woman for him to handle."

Kate laughed out loud. "Don't ever let Sawyer hear you say that."

"I'm looking forward to meeting Lucie."

"J.J. is our other female agent. She's one of the most beautiful women I've ever seen. Picture a young Elizabeth Taylor. Black hair, violet-blue eyes and a petite hourglass figure."

"And she's a Dundee agent?"

"When you meet her, don't let her looks fool you. She's a black belt in karate, is proficient in every weapon imaginable and she rides a Harley."

"I can't wait to meet Lucie and J.J. Are there any rules that say Dundee agents can't date each other?"

"Not that I know of. And it has happened…agents forming personal relationships, but mostly friendships and seldom romances."

"What about you, Kate, are you interested in romance?"

Taken aback by his question, Kate gaped at him, her eyes wide and round. "Are you…" She motioned back and forth between them with her hand. "You and me?"

"Sure. Why not? Unless you patch things up with your ex."

"That's not going to happen."

"Why not? You're still hung up on the guy, aren't you?"

"Maybe I am, but that doesn't mean we'll ever patch things up. Besides, why would you be interested in a romance with me, if you think I still care about Trent?"

"I said romance, not love and marriage." Moran's sly smile gave her the impression he was only halfway joking with her.

"In your language romance translates to sex, right?"

The waitress cleared her throat as she approached with a tray of food. She placed the dishes down in front of Kate and Moran, then asked, "Will there be anything else?"

Kate shook her head.

"No, thanks. We're fine," Moran replied.

"Under different circumstances, you and I might be perfect for each other," Kate told him once the waitress was out of earshot. "Perfect on a temporary basis that is. We're both in the same predicament, romantically speaking."

"How do you figure that?" Moran spread his paper napkin across one knee and picked up his fork.

"Anything we had between us would be friendship and maybe sex, but we're both in love with ghosts from the past, aren't we?"

Moran's hand grasping the fork stopped midair and for the longest moment he didn't move or speak, then finally he laid his fork down and looked at Kate. "I take that to mean you're still in love with your ex or at least with the memory of him. But don't jump to any conclusions where I'm concerned."

"I know you big, strong tough guys don't like to talk about feelings, but it's plain to me that you're pining away for a lost love. It's a matter of it takes-one-to-know-one. I've never loved anyone except Trent and seeing him again, being with him, has gotten me confused. I don't know if I'm in love with the man or with the memory."

"Don't you think you owe it to yourself to find out? You're here with me when you'd rather be with him. Stop running away. Sooner or later, you're going to have to face whatever it is that's happening between you two. And if one of the abduction ring girls turns out to be your daughter, you two won't be able to walk away from each other and never look back."

"You're a very smart man, Dante Moran. So why is it that you can give me such good advice and apparently aren't able to solve your own problems?"

"Look, Kate, I know you mean well and I appreciate your concern, but you don't know anything about me…or about my past."

"So tell me."

"It's not in my nature to open a vein and emotionally bleed all over the place."

"Just tell me one thing and I'll stop badgering you. I promise."

"What do you want to know?" he asked.

"Am I right—is there someone from your past that you can't forget, someone you're still in love with?"

"No more questions if I give you an answer?"

She nodded.

"Yes."

"Yes, what?"

"Yes, there's someone from my past."

Curiosity almost got the best of her, but Kate somehow managed not to pursue the matter. After all, she had promised him, hadn't she? Besides, digging into Moran's past could only temporarily divert her from her own situation with Trent. Moran had been right when he'd said that sooner or later she had to face whatever was happening between Trent and her.

Kate lifted her fork, stirred her salad to equally distribute the honey-mustard dressing, and speared a sizable chunk of mixed greens and sliced grilled chicken. Moran dug into his chicken and dressing, eating heartily. Neither said much while they ate, just a comment now and again on the food and how surprisingly good the coffee was considering the restaurant was an inexpensive diner.

As they finished off their meal and worked on their third cups of coffee, Kate glanced at her watch. Eight forty-five. She really should have called Trent. He was probably wondering about her, maybe even worrying about her. *He has your cell number,* she told herself. *He could call you.* But why should he? Hadn't she all but told him she wanted him out of her sight?

"You're awfully quiet," Moran said.

"Just thinking."

"About your ex?"

A denial was on the tip of her tongue, but why lie to Moran? She nodded. "Man to woman, what would you do if you were in my shoes?"

"My feet wouldn't fit in your shoes." Moran's lips curved into a smirking grin.

"Dammit, will you be serious."

His smile vanished. He reached across the table and clasped her hand, then focused on her face. "If I were in your shoes, I'd go to the guy, tell him how I felt and then drag him off to the nearest bed and make love all night."

Mouth agape, eyes wide, Kate stared at Moran, utterly surprised by his reply. Of all the things she'd expected him to say, that hadn't been one of them. "If that's how you feel, then why haven't you done just that? Why haven't you—"

"I can't. She's dead."

Kate felt as if she'd been slapped. Hit hard with the painful truth. "Oh, God, I'm sorry. I had no idea. I mean…" *Shut up before you dig yourself in deeper,* an inner voice warned.

Moran picked up the check, then scooted out of the booth and said, "Are you ready?"

She nodded, then got up and followed him. She didn't even protest when he paid for her dinner. They walked in silence to his car.

After they got in the car , he asked, "Where to?"

"Drop me off at the Peabody."

"Going to take my advice?"

"Maybe."

Moran started the engine and backed out of the parking space. And all the while Kate thought about how she'd feel if Trent was dead. She'd be devastated. Even though she hadn't seen him in ten years, in all that time apart, she'd known he was alive and well and possibly even happy. Had she, in her heart of hearts, always believed that someday they might get a second chance? Just as she never gave up hope that Mary Kate was alive and eventually they'd be reunited, had she secretly hoped that she and Trent would get back together?

Trent paced the floor in his suite. It was nearly nine-thirty. Where the hell was she? Why hadn't she had the common courtesy to call him? After they'd given their DNA samples, Kate had all but told him to get out of her sight and leave her the hell alone. He could have protested, could have told her that he wasn't leaving her side, but what good would that have done? They'd have wound up in an argument and he didn't want that. Those last few months when their marriage had been dying, that's all they'd done—argue. Day and night. About everything. About anything. It had been easier to stay angry and fight and fume than to face the agonizing pain that had been eating them both alive.

When Kate had suffered a nervous breakdown right after Mary Kate's abduction, he'd done all he could to take care of her, to comfort her, but she'd rejected him time and time again. After a while it became too difficult to endure yet one more rejection. She'd turned away from him, neither wanting nor needing him. At least that was the way it had seemed to him. Instead of clinging to each other, sharing their sorrow, they'd each retreated into their own private hell. When Kate had asked him for a divorce, he'd agreed without a word of protest. His gut instincts had told him he would regret his decision not to fight for his marriage. At the time not only had he been numb with grief over Mary Kate's disappearance, but his damn masculine pride had gotten in the way. A man doesn't hold on to a woman who no longer wants him.

The only problem was that he'd still wanted his wife. He'd wanted her on the day their divorce became final. He'd wanted her a year later. And two years later.

What about ten years later? he asked himself.

The door opened and Kate walked in, her cheeks flushed from the nighttime chill. "It's freezing out there. It's already twenty-eight degrees and feels more like eighteen."

She shrugged out of her coat, then removed her knit gloves and hat and stuffed them into her coat pocket. "Ooh, it's toasty warm in here."

He wanted to rant at her, to demand to know where she'd been, what she'd been doing, and who she'd been with all this time. Moran? Had she been with the sleek, handsome FBI agent since this morning?

"Have you had dinner?" he asked. He'd grabbed a quick lunch in the *Capriccio* Restaurant there in the hotel. He hadn't eaten a bite since.

"Yes, thanks. Moran and I—"

"You had dinner with Moran?"

"At the River City Café." Kate moved slowly toward her bedroom. "It's not far from the FBI field office."

"You and Moran seem to be awfully friendly." *That's it, act like a jealous husband! Remember, you do not want to get into an argument with her.*

"He's a nice guy." Kate halted by her bedroom door. "He has bent some rules and regulations for me because—"

"Because he's got the hots for you." Trent stomped across the room toward her. "God, Kate, I thought you were smarter than you used to be about people, that you weren't as naive. Moran's being nice and helpful because he wants to get in your pants."

Kate slapped him. Her open palm hit squarely against his left cheek. He wasn't sure who was the most startled by her action—him or her. She stared at him in shock. He rubbed his stinging cheek.

"I—I'm sorry, Trent. I didn't mean to do that. It was a knee-jerk reaction."

He rubbed his cheek for a couple more seconds, then eased his hand to his side. "It's okay. I deserved it. That was jealousy you heard talking."

She tilted her head to one side and stared at him. "You're jealous?"

Trent grimaced. "Yeah. It's those old feelings we talked about. That leftover lust."

"Moran and I had dinner together. That's all."

"I don't have a right to be jealous and I know it, but—"

Kate dropped her coat to the floor and moved toward Trent, closing the three-foot gap between them. He held his breath as she came near. "What are we going to do about it? About those old feelings? About that leftover lust?"

Using every ounce of willpower he possessed he balled his hands into fists and managed to stop himself from grabbing her. "What do you think we should do?"

She lifted her arms up and around his neck, then pressed her body intimately against his. "I think we should diffuse the ticking time bomb."

His sex grew hard and heavy. He tightened and released his balled fists. Sweat popped out on his upper lip. "Having sex could turn out to be a big mistake."

"Yes, it could, but it might also relieve all this tension between us. Afterward, we could find out that the only thing left between us really was just some unresolved feelings from the past. We have to do something. We can't go on this way. I'm willing to risk making a big mistake, if you are."

His willpower vanished. With his body fast taking control, his rational thoughts became fewer and fewer. Trent reached down, cupped her buttocks and lifted her up and against his erection. When she whimpered, he lowered his head and claimed her mouth. She clung to him, her breasts crushed against his chest, her mound pressing into his pulsing sex.

"If you're having any second thoughts, you'd better tell me now." He swept her up into his arms and carried her through the lounge and into his bedroom. Without missing a beat, he laid her on the bed and came down over her, his mouth still devouring hers, his hands ripping at her clothes.

Seven

Kate couldn't remember the last time she'd felt this way—on fire, burning with an all-consuming desire. She'd known other men, had enjoyed the sex and the friendship they'd shared, but only with Trent had she experienced true passion. A passion of the senses, of the heart, of the very soul. Swept away by an unexplainable hunger, by a need so strong that it overpowered everything else, she surrendered herself to her primeval needs. Her body instantly recognized Trent's touch, his smell, his taste. And aroused beyond all reason, she responded instinctively. It had always been like this for them—no holding back, giving and taking with every breath, no rational thought, only an overwhelming desire for appeasement.

She could stop him. It wasn't too late. Not yet. She should call a halt, shouldn't she? This was madness. But heaven help them both, it was such sweet madness.

She had managed to unbutton his shirt while he'd yanked her sweater over her head. As they kissed, they tossed and tumbled on the bed. When she was breathless, Trent ended the kiss and lifted his head. Panting, her heart racing, she stared up into his brown eyes, shimmering with dark, uncontrollable desire. She reached out and touched his face. The light beard stubble scraped her fingertips like a fine sandpaper. Trent rose to his knees, drawing her up with him so that they faced each other. Gripping her shoulders, he let his gaze travel over her face, down her throat, and across her breasts. He reached behind her and unhooked her bra, then eased the straps down her arms and slipped the beige-satin garment off. His hot gaze and the cool air attacked her skin, tightening her nipples to pebble-hard points.

She rubbed her fingers over his chest, her nails raking his tiny male nipples and inching through the vee of curly dark hair. She loved the feel of him. The hardness of his muscular body and the softness of his chest hair. Touching him titillated her, bringing long-dormant emotions to the surface.

After cupping both of her breasts, he flicked his thumbs over her nipples. A tingling, clenching sensation shot through her, sensitizing her breasts and moistening her femininity. The achiness between her thighs grew more intense by the moment. Her body tightened and released. The process repeated itself, preparing her, moistening her.

Wanting, needing, hungry for all of him, Kate undid his belt and unbuttoned his slacks, then lowered the zipper. Her movements eager, yet patiently deliberate, she tugged on his trousers, bringing them down over his hips. He pulled away from her and stood so that he could shrug out of his pants. She scooted to the edge of the bed, reached out and jerked down his black briefs, but they caught on his impressive erection. Gently she eased the material over his sex and down his legs. He kicked the briefs aside, sending them to join his discarded slacks.

An unbearable yearning urged her into action. Still on her knees at the edge of the bed, she grasped his hips and pulled him closer. Her right hand circled him. Caressed. Pumped. Trent groaned. Kate smiled.

He reached down and eased her hand away, then dragged her off the bed and onto her feet to stand in front of him. With less finesse and more urgency than she had displayed in disrobing him, he removed her slacks and panties, leaving her completely naked. With labored breaths, sexual hunger raging inside them, they came together. Bare breasts to hairy chest. Flat belly to hard, pulsating sex. They kissed, tender need soon turning to heated passion. They touched each other, hands petting, clutching, exploring.

He rubbed her buttocks as if he was feeling and appreciating the finest silk. While she deposited damp, adoring kisses on his chest, he forked his fingers through her hair and grasped tightly. Yanking her head up so that she faced him, he stared at her for a millisecond. After releasing his tenacious hold on her head, he pushed her back onto the bed. Before she had a chance to catch her breath, he positioned her hips on the edge, then dropped to his knees, parted her thighs and placed her legs on either side of his hips.

"Trent?"

"Shh."

He kissed first one inner thigh and then the other, repeating the back and forth process from just above her knees to the apex of her legs. Trent was the only man who'd ever realized that her inner thighs were an extremely sexually sensitive area of her body. He added long, wet licks to the kisses, interchanging the two actions until Kate thought she'd climax on the spot. But when she came close to losing it, Trent changed tactics. He kissed her intimately. She shivered. When his tongue touched her throbbing nub, she cried out, pleasure rippling through every nerve in her body.

As he continued loving her with his mouth and tongue, he reached up over her stomach and tweaked her nipples, adding pressure to the pulsating tension drumming through her body. Minutes later, she came. Crying out, undulating her hips, she went wild. And Trent continued, not letting up until she was totally spent, until he'd drained every ounce of satisfaction from her release. As tiny aftershocks fluttered through her, Trent swung her around into the bed and joined her, coming down over her, straddling her hips.

She reached out for him, touching his sex. He shuddered. She longed to give him the kind of pleasure he'd given her. Without asking his permission, she shoved him over onto his back. He flopped over and without protest, let her take charge.

"You don't have to—"

"I want to," she told him.

She kissed his lips, his chin and his throat. Then she licked a moist line from shoulder to shoulder, across his chest and down his belly. With tender caresses and long, all-day-sucker licks, she put her desire into action. He threaded his fingers through her hair and urged her to take him into her mouth. She gave him exactly what he wanted. The taste of him excited her. Giving herself over completely to mindless, exhilarating wantonness, she brought him to an earth-shattering release.

Trent roared, the sound loud and animalistic. As fulfillment wound itself around him, shaking him from the inside out, he pulled her up and over his damp, hot body, until their lips met once again. When they kissed deeply and their tongues mated, they tasted themselves as well as each other. He wrapped his arms around her and held her close. Neither of them spoke, just lay there for endless moments. Finally, Kate shivered.

"Are you cold?" he asked.

"A little chilly," she replied.

He slipped off the bed and pulled down the cover, allowing her to crawl beneath the sheet, blanket and spread before he slid in beside her. She snuggled close to him. He eased one arm under her neck so that her head rested on his shoulder.

"Trent?"

"Mmm, hmm?"

What should she say? Should she admit that she still cared about him? Or should she act as if their having sex was no big deal? While she was trying to form the right sentence, to put together the correct words, the telephone rang. Kate tensed. Trent grunted.

"Any chance that's Moran?" Trent asked as he reached toward the phone on the bedside table.

"Not unless there's been a major new development in the case."

Trent yanked the receiver from the hook. "Yeah?"

Kate felt an instant change in Trent. He eased his arm away, leaving her head resting on his pillow, and then he rose to a sitting position.

"No, I'm sorry. I forgot about calling. It's been a long day and—"

"Who is it?" Kate spoke quietly, more mouthing the question than uttering it out loud.

Trent shook his head.

"No, we don't know much more than we did. We gave DNA samples for testing that will compare our DNA to the three little girls. Look, would you hold on a minute? I want to change phones." Trent laid the phone down on the table, slipped out of bed, walked over to the closet and removed a robe.

Kate watched him as he put on the robe and walked into the lounge, not once looking back at her or speaking to her. Had Aunt Mary Belle called him? Probably. But why did he need privacy to talk to his aunt? What could he have to say to her that he couldn't say in front of Kate?

It's not Aunt Mary Belle, an inner voice told her. *It's Molly Stoddard, his almost fiancé.* And Trent's feeling guilty because he just made love with his ex-wife. She eyed the phone lying on the bedside table. The temptation to pick up the receiver and listen nearly got the best of her.

Don't do it, she warned herself. She reached out, lifted the receiver and set it down on the base. Temptation resisted. She breathed a sigh of relief.

Kate got out of bed, gathered up her clothes and marched through the lounge, not even acknowledging Trent's presence as she rushed to her bedroom. She slammed the door as loud as she could. There, let him think whatever he wants to about that.

Well, hell, what had she expected to happen? Even if Trent's lady love hadn't called tonight, where'd she think that sexual interlude she'd shared with him would lead? Trent has built a new life for himself back in Prospect. He has a career he loves and a woman he wants to build a future with, a woman his aunt knows is good enough for him. Kate didn't even know Molly Stoddard, but right this minute, she hated the woman.

* * *

"Yes, Kate and I are getting along all right," Trent said, realizing that was the understatement of the decade. They were getting along better than all right. Hell, they'd just shared some really great oral sex. And he didn't have a doubt in his mind that Kate had enjoyed it as much as he had.

"I know this must be terribly difficult for you, darling, but once you learn if one of those poor children is or is not Mary Kate, then you can move on," Molly said. "After all, before this happened, you'd been certain your daughter was dead. And if she isn't one of the little girls, then your assumption has probably been right all along. On the other hand, if she is one of the girls, then you and your ex-wife can hardly take her away from the only parents she's ever known."

"Yes, of course, you're right." He didn't want to discuss this with Molly. Not tonight. Maybe not ever. Although she was a parent—a good parent—she couldn't begin to understand how he felt. Only Kate understood. Only Kate felt the same anguish.

Trent eyed the closed door to Kate's bedroom. Only halfway listening to Molly, he thought about his ex-wife, about what had just happened between them. He could still see her, totally naked and toting her discarded clothes, tromping angrily through the lounge, ignoring him completely. And he could still hear the door slamming. She was mad as hell and wanted him to know it.

Damn! She had every right to be upset with him. Why had he acted like an idiot?

"Trent? Trent!"

"Huh?"

"Have you heard a word I've said?"

"Sorry, Molly, my mind wandered."

"Something's wrong. What is it? Tell me. If I can help you, I want to—"

"If you really want to help…" Damn, damn, damn! He was torn between Molly and the truth. He wanted to hold on to Molly, on to the plans he'd been making for a peaceful, contented future with her and her children. But how could he do that to her—keep her dangling on a string while he sorted out his feelings for Kate? And God knew those feelings were about as complicated and confusing as feelings could get.

He wanted Kate now as much as ever. The lust factor between them hadn't diminished one iota. But did he love Kate? Maybe. A part of him would always love her. The real question was did they have a future together, with or without Mary Kate?

"Molly, I owe you honesty," Trent said.

"I'm not sure I like the sound of that."

"Kate and I…that is, we—"

"The ghost of marriage past has risen its alluring head," Molly said. "Is that it?"

"In a way."

"It was bound to happen. Kate was the love of your life, just as Peter was the love of my life. I can't say that I'm not disappointed. I'd hoped we could build a good, solid life together. But in all honesty, if it were possible for Peter to walk back into my life this very minute, I'd run into his arms and never let him go."

"It's not quite the same for Kate and me. When Peter died, you two were still very much in love. Kate and I could barely look at each other by the time our divorce became final."

"Oh, Trent, don't you think I've always known, even without Miss Mary Belle telling me?"

"What are you talking about? What did my aunt tell you?"

"She told me that you'd be in love with Kate Malone to the day you die."

Why was it that Molly's statement hit him like a sledgehammer? Because he was afraid it might be true? "Aunt Mary Belle over-romanticized the situation."

"Look, Trent, I'm not going anywhere," Molly told him. "There isn't anyone else in my life. If you can't renew things with Kate or find out you don't want to, then I'll still be here in Prospect waiting for you. And if you two wind up getting back together, I'll understand. Who knows, I might even like Kate."

"You're a remarkable woman," Trent said.

"Not really. I'm just envious that you might get a second chance with the love of your life."

Trent didn't know how to respond to that, so he said nothing.

"Take care of yourself," Molly told him. "Call me when you get back to Prospect."

"I will. I promise."

Trent hung up, tightened the belt on his robe and marched to Kate's door. He knocked. No response. He knocked again, several times.

"Kate?"

"Go away."

"Kate, we need to talk."

"No, we don't."

"Yes, we do." Trent tried the knob and found the door locked. "Dammit, Kate, don't be this way."

"I do not want to see you or talk to you. Not tonight. Just leave me alone. If we have to talk, we can do it in the morning. I'm tired and I want to go to sleep."

"Look, I'm sorry. Is that what you want to hear? I

handled Molly's call all wrong. I should have told you she was the caller and I should have told her I'd call her back later. It's just that she caught me off guard and I felt odd talking to her while I was lying in bed with you."

"You felt guilty. Admit it. You'd just cheated on her and—"

"Dammit, Kate, don't put it that way. Molly isn't my wife. She's not even my fiancé."

Silence.

Trent lifted his fist to the door, but stopped himself just short of knocking again. He leaned his head against the door and groaned quietly. "Molly knows that you and I have issues we need to work through. She's very understanding. She's not jealous or anything like that."

The door swung open so quickly that Trent almost lost his balance. Hands on hips, Kate stood there and glared at him. "Did you tell her that we'd—"

"No, I did not tell her. But it wouldn't have mattered if I had. She's not the type to—"

"Be jealous? Throw a fit? Come to Memphis and rip my hair out by the roots?" Kate lifted one hand and pointed her index finger in Trent's face. "If she isn't jealous, then she doesn't love you. If I were *practically* your fiancé and you went away with your ex-wife for any reason whatsoever, I'd be jealous as hell. And if I even suspected that you'd made love with her, I'd want to scratch her eyes out."

"That's the difference between you and Molly," Trent admitted. "If you were *practically* my fiancé, you'd be madly in love with me. Molly isn't. Unless you've changed a great deal, loving with all your heart is the only way you know how to love. It was always all or nothing for you."

"Molly isn't in love with you and you want to marry her?" Kate stared at him quizzically as she eased her hands off her hips. "Forget I asked. It's none of my business." Kate turned around and started to close the door.

Trent stuck his foot over the threshold to prevent her from shutting the door. Kate glanced over her shoulder, her eyes questioning his intentions. "I'm going on forty. I want a normal, ordinary existence, a family, someone with whom I can share my life. I like and admire Molly. She feels the same about me."

"In other words, you're willing to settle." Kate pivoted around slowly.

Their gazes met and locked.

"Yes, I suppose I am."

"Well, good for you. When we find out what we need to know about Mary Kate, you can go right back to Prospect and marry Molly Stoddard and live the rest of your lives in peaceful, uneventful mediocrity. No disagreeing, no arguing, no ups and down, just smooth sailing on smooth waters. No waves." Kate indicated an even line with the movement of her hand gliding through the air. "But the downside of that is no passion, no to-die-for love and no blow-the-top-of-your-head-off sex that touches not just your body, but your heart, too. And even your soul."

Kate turned her back on him again and tried to close the door. He remained unmoving.

"To have that kind of love once in a lifetime is more than most of us can expect," Trent said. "And when you've had it and lost it, the best you can do is settle for less."

She stood there, her back to him. He wanted to grab her tense shoulders, drag her into his arms and carry her back to his bed for a repeat performance, but he managed—just barely—to keep his hands off her.

"I'll never settle for less. I still want it all. And if I can't have it all, I'll take nothing."

She tried again to close the door. This time Trent moved his foot and allowed her to accomplish her goal. He stood there staring at the door for quite some time, his mind reeling with a jumble of thoughts. About Kate. About Molly. About the future.

Eight

Dante Moran called at seven-thirty. Kate had been awake since six o'clock, but she hadn't ventured from her room. She'd called herself a coward, a fool and a hussy, not necessarily in that order. A coward for not wanting to face Trent this morning. A hussy and a fool for allowing herself to give in to temptation last night.

Maybe she should add judgmental bitch to that list. After all, what right did she have to judge Trent? If he wanted to settle for a marriage without passion, was that so wrong? For her—definitely yes. But maybe not for Trent. The old Trent, the man she'd fallen in love with and married would never have been satisfied with less than everything. The new Trent—she didn't really know him, did she?

"Kate are you there?" Moran asked.

"Sorry, just gathering wool."

"Did I wake you?"

"No, I've been up for quite a while. But it is early, so why are you calling?"

"To let you know that it doesn't look as if we'll be able to set up a meeting between the adoptive parents and the biological parents."

"What? Why not?"

"None of the adoptive parents are willing to attend a meeting."

"I see." A gut-tightening sense of disappointment hit Kate.

"You can't blame them. Not really," Moran said. "They're all scared to death, afraid they might lose their child. Right or wrong, they see the biological parents as enemies."

"I can understand why they'd feel that way. After all, they're as much victims in this horrific situation as we are. And if the shoe was on the other foot, I'd probably feel the way they do."

"I called you first," Moran told her. "We'll be letting the others know later today."

"Thanks."

"Not all my news is bad."

"How's that?" she asked.

"The adoptive parents did agree to send recent photographs of the girls via e-mail attachments. And one is even sending several photos of their child, dating from infancy."

Kate's heart skipped a beat as her hopes shot sky-high. "From infancy? If we saw a picture of our child as an infant, we'd recognize her immediately."

"I don't know why I told you about that. Dammit, Kate, she's not one of the two with type O-positive blood."

Her sky-high hopes nosedived. "But we will see photos of the other two girls, right?"

Would she know her own daughter from a photograph? Or would her eager heart see something that wasn't there—a resemblance to her or to Trent that would be only in her imagination?

"Absolutely. All of you will get copies. We're expecting those photos this morning. I'll phone you the minute we get all three sets."

"Hey, Moran, you know where all three girls live, don't you?"

"Yeah, we know." A slight hesitation. A deep breath. "But don't ask me to give you the addresses. I can't bend the rules that much."

"Could you tell me if they're close?" she asked. "Just tell me the states they're in."

"The two with type O-positive blood are within three hours of Memphis," he told her. "One's in Mississippi and the other in Alabama. And that's all I can tell you at this point. I'm sorry, Kate, I'd tell you everything I know, but—"

"It's okay. Really. I wouldn't want to get you fired before you have a chance to resign."

He chuckled. "I'll let you know the minute the pictures come in."

"I'll be right here waiting."

She'd no sooner hung up the phone than Trent knocked at her bedroom door. She knew it was Trent. Who else would it be? She had showered and dressed when she first got up, then made coffee and downed every drop the four-cup pot held.

Bracing herself to see Trent, she flung open the door. He stood there looking much too handsome, his dark hair neatly combed, his face freshly saved and wearing jeans and a cable-knit navy-blue sweater over a light blue button-down shirt.

"I ordered breakfast," he said, his voice neutral, neither warm nor cold. Not friendly. Not hostile. "It just arrived. I hope a ham and cheese omelette with whole wheat toast and coffee suits you."

"It suits me just fine. Thank you." It touched her heart that he'd remembered the only way she would eat eggs when she was pregnant with Mary Kate was in an omelette. And her favorite had been ham and cheese.

Before she entered the lounge, he turned away from her and walked over to the table. Whatever tension their lovemaking had diffused had now been replaced with even more friction—sexual tension, a touch of anger and a hint of awkwardness.

When she approached, he held her chair for her and assisted her in sitting. She looked up over her shoulder and offered him a smile. He nodded, but didn't return the smile. After he sat across from her and removed the covers from their plates, she took a deep breath, in an effort to bolster her courage, and looked right at him.

"About last night," she said.

"What about last night? Are you referring to our lovemaking or Molly's phone call or my stupidity or your overreacting to—"

"All of the above."

With his gaze glued to hers, he nodded.

"Look, Trent, I'm the one who should apologize. I shouldn't have said some of the things I did. You have every right to marry whomever you please for whatever reason."

"I'm not going to marry Molly."

Her heart fluttered like a captive butterfly. "You're not?"

"No, I'm not. I thought a great deal about what you said and I realized you were right. I'd tried so hard to forget what it was like between us when we first got married that I'd actually halfway convinced myself that I could live without passion in my marriage. But I can't. Making love with you last night proved that to me. You and I may no longer be in love, but God help us, the passion hasn't faded one bit, has it?"

Her breath caught in her throat and for a moment she couldn't speak. She desperately wanted to touch him, to feel his flesh beneath her fingertips. *But I do love you, Trent. I always have and always will. Why couldn't she tell him? If she admitted her true feelings, maybe he would, too. But what if he doesn't love you? What if passion really is all he feels?*

"The passion certainly was there last night," she said. "In spades."

He smiled then. A warm, genuine smile that showed in his eyes. "May I ask who called you a few minutes ago or is that none of my business?"

"It was Special Agent Moran." Kate poured coffee into her cup, then added a generous amount of cream. "None of the adoptive parents will meet with us, but they are e-mailing photographs of the girls."

Trent lifted his cup and sipped the coffee. "I suppose I can understand why they don't want to meet with us. If I were in their place, I'd be out of my mind with fear. I feel sorry for everyone involved—the adoptive parents as well as us birth parents. We're all in a no-win situation."

"If one of the girls is Mary Kate, we aren't going to take her away from the people who've raised her, are we?" Kate needed him to be strong for both of them because she wasn't sure if once she found out one of the girls was her daughter, she'd be able to do the right thing for Mary Kate. "We can't do that to her, no matter how difficult it is for us."

When Kate lifted her cup, she had to set it back down immediately because her hand trembled so badly. Damn! She swallowed the tears lodged in her throat.

Trent set his cup on the table. "No, we can't do that to her, no matter how much we'd like to take her with us, shower her with love and never let her go."

"I have to see her. I have to believe in my heart that leaving her with her adoptive family is the right thing to do."

"We both need that. Whatever happens, it's going to be difficult for us."

She looked down at her lap, avoiding direct eye contact with Trent as she spoke. "Moran has the addresses for all three girls. I hope to sneak a peek at them when we go to his office this morning. If I manage to get those addresses, will you go with me to see the girls? Like the other birth mothers, I keep thinking that if I saw her, I'd recognize her."

"Call me a fool, but yes, I'll go with you," Trent said. "We'll have to be very discreet. We can't let any one of the three girls or their parents see us and realize why we're there. We're in agreement on that, right? Even if you think you recognize Mary Kate, you won't—"

"There are only two girls we need to see. Only two have type O-positive blood." She lifted her gaze to meet Trent's. "Moran told me yesterday and I'm sorry I didn't share that information with you immediately."

Trent glanced away, a sad look in his eyes. "Even if you're sure one of the two girls is our daughter, you won't speak to her or alert her to our presence, will you?"

"I promise that no matter how much I want to grab her and hug her and kiss her, I won't do anything to make our presence known. We can watch her from a distance. But I have to see these girls. I can't wait. I've been waiting nearly twelve years. I feel as if I'm on the verge of shattering into a million pieces."

"I know how you feel. Believe me, I know."

"Let's not wait for Moran to call back," Kate said. "As soon as we finish breakfast, let's go on over to the field office. Okay?"

"Sure thing. But you have to eat first. You're too thin, Kate. You've skipped too many meals lately, haven't you? You've always been that way, unable to eat when you're upset and worried."

"You know me too well." She offered him a half-hearted smile, then lifted her cup to her lips.

Robin Elliott lived in Corinth, Mississippi, with her parents, Susan and Neal Elliott, and her younger brother, Scottie, who was also adopted. Christa Farrell lived in Sheffield, Alabama, with her paternal grandmother, Brenda Farrell. She'd been adopted by Brenda's son, Rick, and his wife, Jean, who'd been killed in a plane crash when they'd flown to Barbados for their anniversary six years ago.

While Trent kept the Bentley humming at sixty-five miles an hour along Highway 72, which would take them all the way from Memphis to Corinth, Kate continuously looked at the copies of the two photographs Moran had issued to the four sets of biological parents. While Trent had kept Moran busy with questions, Kate had rifled through the paperwork on Moran's desk until she found the information on the adoptive parents and their daughters, including their addresses. She'd had easy access to the info, leading her to believe that Moran had known what she'd do and had purposely left that specific file folder on his desk for her to find.

Kate studied the first photograph, a school picture of Robin Elliott. The child was lovely, her features perfect. A pink satin clasp held the bangs of her short blond hair to one side. It was difficult to make out the exact color of her eyes, but they appeared to be a light brown, flecked with green. Hazel brown. Trent's aunt Mary Belle had hazel-brown eyes.

The information attached to the picture stated that Robin would celebrate her twelfth birthday in three weeks. She was in the sixth grade, an average student, who excelled at gymnastics and was a mini-midget football cheerleader. From all reports, she was happy, healthy and well-adjusted.

Kate flipped that photo over and stared at the picture of the second little girl with type-O blood. A pair of large brown eyes looked up at Kate. Eyes as dark as Trent's. She wore her long brown hair in dog ears, green bows attached to each in a shade that perfectly matched her sweater. Christa Farrell was a pretty child, but her features weren't perfect. Her lips were too full and her nose just a tad too big. And a smattering of freckles dotted her nose and cheekbones. Kate had been cursed with freckles as a child, but makeup and staying out of the sun kept her few remaining freckles under control.

Christa, who would celebrate her twelfth birthday in two weeks, was a straight-A student, a real little bookworm, but she wasn't social by nature and had very few friends. A quiet, introverted child, she preferred the company of her grandmother and other adults to children her own age. The girl was healthy and exceptionally bright, but had been emotionally fragile since her parents' deaths when she was only six.

Kate laid the pictures side by side in her lap. *Is one of you Mary Kate? If so, why don't I know you? Why can't I look at your face and instantly recognize you as mine?* She found herself drawn first to Robin and then to Christa, for different reasons. She saw herself and Trent in both girls. Christa had Mary Kate's brown eyes, but Robin had her blond hair.

"You're going to wear those photos out before we get to Corinth." Trent gave her a quick sidelong glance.

"I know, but I can't seem to stop looking at them." Kate sighed heavily. "One of these girls could very easily be our Mary Kate. Why don't I recognize my own child? Maybe neither of them is Mary Kate."

"You're driving yourself crazy and that's not doing either of us any good. The DNA test results will be back soon and we'll know for sure."

"I suppose we should have waited for those test results and not gone off on some wild-goose chase, but I swear I think I'd have lost my mind if we'd stayed in Memphis."

"Make that both of us," Trent told her. "Even if turns out that neither of these girls is Mary Kate, we're no worse off than we were before, except for getting our hopes up. I was getting antsy myself just waiting around."

"How long until we get to Corinth?"

"We're less than twenty miles away."

Kate sucked in a deep breath, then let it out in a long, relieved rush. "1212 Oak Hill Drive." She checked her wristwatch. "Robin should be coming home from school in about thirty minutes. Maybe we can catch a glimpse of her then."

"Remember, we aren't going to do anything to alert her or her family of our presence."

"I remember."

* * *

Trent did his best to stay calm, to remain in control, for Kate's sake as well as his own. They had parked the Bentley in the driveway of a house with a For Sale sign in the yard, only one house down and across the street from 1212 Oak Hill Drive. If anyone became suspicious of them, they could say they were shopping for a new home and stopped to check out the place at 1215. The frigid winter wind chilled him to the bone, making him glad he'd worn his heavy wool coat and leather gloves.

Feigning interest in the house and grounds, they tromped around in the yard and peeked in the windows, all the while keeping an eye out for any action at 1212 Oak Hill Drive.

Minutes ticked by. The longer they stayed outside, the more wicked the wind and colder the temperature seemed.

"Why don't we get back in the car for a few minutes and warm ourselves," Trent suggested. "I don't known about you, but I'm freezing."

Hugging herself in an effort to get warm, Kate nodded. "Let's go. I think my feet and hands are frostbitten, and I know my nose is."

Just as they reached the Bentley, Trent noticed a late-model Buick pull into the driveway at 1212. "Look, Kate."

She halted at his side and looked across the street. Gasping, she grabbed his hand. His heartbeat drummed loudly inside his head. Was it possible that he was on the verge of seeing his daughter?

A tall, blond woman emerged from the Buick, quickly followed by two children. A boy who looked to be about eight hopped out of the back seat, a book bag hanging loosely off one shoulder. The passenger side door opened and a thin, willowy young girl in jeans and a brown leather jacket emerged.

Kate squeezed his hand. They moved in unison to the end of the driveway and onto the sidewalk. Trying as best they could to act nonchalantly, they stared at Robin Elliott. She was a beguilingly beautiful child. When she laughed at something her brother said to her as they ran toward the front door, Trent's heart skipped a beat. Her smile reminded him of Kate's smile. And with her blond hair and willowy build, she looked a bit like the pictures of Kate when she was a kid. Was it possible that Robin was really Mary Kate?

"She looks so happy," Kate said.

"She is happy. That's obvious."

"Do you think…could you tell if she's anything like Mary Kate was as an infant?"

"She's got blond hair, although it's a honey blond now. And her smile reminds me of yours. But maybe I'm grasping at straws, wanting her to be ours."

"I don't know if she's Mary Kate," Kate admitted. "I want her to be, but I don't feel it." She laid her left hand over her heart. "I don't sense it, in here."

They continued staring at Robin until she disappeared inside her house. Then they stood on the sidewalk for quite some time, unable to speak or move. Oddly enough it was Kate who finally put an end to their senseless vigil.

"Let's go," Kate said. "It's highly unlikely she'll come back outside in weather like this."

"You're right. There's no sense waiting around for another glimpse, is there?"

They hurried to the Bentley. Once inside, Trent started the engine to warm the interior, then turned to Kate. "We can be in Sheffield in a little over an hour. It's only about fifty or sixty miles from here."

Kate checked her watch. "Christa Farrell goes to the

public library every day after school. Her grandmother works there. We should be able to make it to Sheffield before the library closes."

Trent reached over and ran the back of his gloved hand down Kate's pink cheek. "Are you all right?"

"Yeah, I'm okay."

"Have you thought ahead?" he asked. "Have you thought about what you'll do if neither Robin nor Christa turns out to be Mary Kate?"

"I'll handle it if it happens." Her gaze met his. "You have to know that I'll never give up looking for our child."

He sat there quietly for a few minutes. *Tell her how you feel,* an inner voice advised. *Let her know she isn't alone in her quest.* "If it turns out that way—that neither girl is Mary Kate—I want to help you to continue searching. I want us to keep looking for our daughter together."

Kate clenched her teeth and turned her head. He sensed that she was struggling with her emotions, making a valiant effort not to cry. Damn! He knew exactly how she felt.

Kate's nerves were raw by the time they pulled into the parking place in front of the Sheffield library in the middle of the downtown area. A small town, with many buildings empty, Sheffield looked forlorn, but there was evidence of revitalization here and there. All the way up Highway 72 as they bypassed Iuka, zoomed through Cherokee and hit every red light in Tuscumbia, Kate kept studying Robin Elliott's photo. Images of the laughing child flashed through Kate's mind. If Robin was Mary Kate, then why didn't she feel it in her mother's heart? *Maybe she's not yours,* an inner voice said. *Maybe Christa Farrell is Mary Kate. But what if you see her and don't recognize her as yours?*

"So, do we wait here for the library to close or do we go in?" Trent asked.

Go inside? Oh, God, could she do that? Could she be that close to Christa and remain at a distance? Wouldn't she be tempted to speak to the child, to study her like a bug under a microscope?

"Let's go inside," Kate said.

"Are you sure?"

Kate nodded.

"We can't stare and we can't talk to her. Understood?"

"Yes, I understand."

They exited the Bentley and went inside the library, which was small enough that they could scan the entire interior in one sweeping glance. Kate opened her purse and slid the photos inside, then searched again for any sign of Christa. In her second scan, she saw the little girl sitting alone at a table, a book satchel in the chair beside her, an open notebook in front of her and a pencil in her hand.

"There she is," Kate whispered.

Trent followed her line of vision.

"I wish she'd look up so we could see her face better."

"We've got to stop staring at her," Trent said. "Let's pick out a few magazines and take them over to the table next to her."

Kate followed Trent and after they'd chosen several magazines, they headed for the table nearest Christa. When they sat down across from each other, the child lifted her head and looked right at Kate. Christa smiled, but didn't speak. Kate returned the smile. Her stomach muscles tightened when she noted what a deep, chocolate brown the little girl's eyes were. The same color as Trent's.

That doesn't mean she's Mary Kate.

What was probably Christa's homework once again gained her full attention, so Kate and Trent were able to occasionally glance at the child while they pretended interest in the magazines they'd laid out on the table. The more she studied the little girl, the more similarities Kate recognized. She had eyes like Trent. Same color, same intense expression when she worked. And her mouth was generously full—like Trent's. The shape of her face—like a valentine—and the light dusting of freckles were traits inherited from Kate. She had Kate's mother's nose—a tad too big for her little face, but she'd grow into it as her grandmother had.

Damn, Kate, don't do this to yourself. She was looking for things that would make this girl hers. What about her hair? It wasn't blond like Kate's or dark brown like Trent's. No, but it was a light brown, which could well be the blending of their two hair colors. And Christa was slightly plump. She and Trent had both been skinny as kids, as Robin Elliott was. But Kate knew for a fact that Mary Belle Winston had been a plump child.

There you go again, trying to convince yourself that this child is your daughter, Kate told herself. Was she seeing similarities that weren't there? Or was this little girl really Mary Kate? Something deep inside Kate was drawn to this child, but did that mean the girl belonged to her?

"You're staring," Trent whispered as he reached across the table and clasped Kate's trembling hands.

She forced herself to look away from Christa. "Do you see it? Or am I imagining all the similarities?" Kate kept her voice low and soft.

"My eyes and mouth. Your shape face and freckles."

Realizing Trent had recognized the resemblance, too, Kate couldn't stop herself from glancing toward Christa again. Just in time to see the child chewing on her pencil. Kate's heart stopped. Her mother had scolded her throughout her childhood and teens for chewing on her pencil. Sometimes she still caught herself doing it.

Kate swallowed the lump in her throat. Tears gathered in the corners of her eyes.

"We'd better get out of here," Trent said.

Kate nodded. They gathered up their magazines. Nervously clumsy, she accidentally dropped one on the floor. Before she could get it, Christa jumped out of her seat, bent over, picked up the magazine and handed it to Kate. Their gazes met. Kate looked at the child through the tears misting her eyes. Christa smiled again and it was all Kate could do to stop herself from grabbing the little girl and hugging her for dear life.

"Thank you." Kate accepted the magazine.

Trent slipped his arm around Kate's waist to give her much-needed support. She felt as if her knees were going to give way at any minute.

"You're welcome," Christa said.

Before she embarrassed herself by reaching out and touching the child's angelic little face, Trent urged her into motion and all but forced her to walk away. He took her magazines from her once they were near the magazine rack. Within minutes he escorted her out of the library and straight to the car. He opened the passenger door. Kate turned to him, tears trickling down her cheeks.

Trent grabbed her and pulled her into his arms. She clung to him, weeping quietly. He stroked her back. "Don't do this, honey. You'll make yourself sick."

"I know it's crazy, but I think—I feel—that she's Mary Kate."

"Yeah, I know. I know."

"Did you—" Kate gulped down tears. "Did you feel it, too?"

Trent kissed her. Sweet and comforting. Slightly edged with passion.

"Yeah, I felt it, too. But it could be nothing more than wishful thinking on our parts."

"Maybe, but my heart tells me that that little girl in there—" Kate inclined her head toward the library "—is our Mary Kate."

Nine

The next three days were sheer agony for Kate. And she knew they were for Trent, too, although they didn't talk about it much. The waiting was unbearable. Both of them were on edge, their nerves frayed. They alternated between clinging to each other and arguing over nothing. Kate often left the hotel alone during the day and walked for an hour or two, despite the frigid temperatures. All the pent-up energy inside her kept her on the verge of either crying or screaming. And she knew that if she didn't get away from Trent when the tension reached a fever pitch, she'd wind up dragging him off to bed. The sexual tension between them was palpable, pulsating just below the surface twenty-four/seven. Having sex might give them momentary release, but what would the long-term effects be? She couldn't have a temporary sexual relationship with Trent. Leaving him ten years ago had nearly killed her. She would not put herself through that agony a second time.

This morning Trent had been the one to leave their suite, telling her she could reach him by cell phone if she needed him. If she needed him? Heaven help her, she needed him now. Needed him every minute of every day. And that was bad news for her. She'd already allowed herself to become too accustomed to leaning on Trent, depending on him.

This morning had dragged by, as had the previous days, even though she'd done numerous things to keep busy. She'd put a deep-conditioner on her hair, a thirty-minute treatment. She'd tried to watch a TV talk show, had flipped through several magazines and read a couple of chapters in a paperback novel she'd picked up a couple of days ago at a downtown bookstore. She'd even painted her fingernails and toenails. And she'd drunk four cups of Earl Grey!

What now? It was barely noon and she'd already run out of things to do. As she paced around in the lounge, doing her best not to think about the DNA tests or her gut-level reaction to Christa Farrell at the Sheffield library, Kate mulled over her options. She could take another walk, but the truth of the matter was, she didn't know where Trent had gone and didn't want to run into him. The way she felt right now, she might pull him into the nearest dark alley and have her way with him.

Kate laughed. God, she was losing it.

She needed someone to talk to, someone other than Trent. Lucie! That's it, she thought, who better to commiserate with than her best buddy? Kate dialed Lucie's cell phone. She answered on the third ring.

"Evans here."

"Lucie, it's me. Are you busy? In the middle of something?"

"Hey, girl, what's up? Any news?"

"Nothing yet. I'm losing my mind waiting. And on the verge of attacking my ex-husband."

"Attack as in killing him or jumping his bones?"

"The latter."

"Mmm, hmm. So, why don't you?"

Kate wondered how she should reply.

"Oh, don't tell me," Lucie said. "You've already done that, haven't you?"

"Yes," Kate admitted. "And I can't let it happen again."

"Why not? You're both consenting adults."

"Becoming lovers would complicate things too much and the situation is already complicated enough as it is."

"Why don't you just admit that you're still nuts about the guy? Even if he has a fiancé, I'll bet if he knew how you felt—"

"He's not going to marry her. He's not going to propose."

"Hooray and hallelujah. Grab that man while you can."

"Can't risk it. I may be in love, but I'm not so sure about him. It could be just lust for him. And I'm too emotionally fragile right now to lose both Trent and Mary Kate for a second time."

"Ah, hon, what a situation to be in."

"Lucie?"

"Mmm, hmm?"

"I stole the addresses for the two girls with type O-positive blood and Trent and I went to see them." When Lucie let out a long, exaggerated ooh, Kate quickly added, "We saw them, but they didn't know who we were or that we were looking them over. We were very careful. Very discreet."

"And?"

"And we both got similar vibes from the same child. Her name is Christa. I swear, Lucie, I just know she's Mary Kate.

"That had to have been rough on you. On both of you. You must have wanted to grab her and squeeze the life out of her."

"You have no idea. Dammit, what am I going to do if the DNA test proves me right? How can I not claim her?"

"Did you see her with her adoptive parents? I mean, did you get a glimpse of how their relationship is?"

"Christa's adoptive parents died nearly six years ago," Kate said. "She lives with her grandmother."

"Won't that simplify matters? Doesn't that make it easier for you and Trent to get custody of her?"

"It might, but how do we in good conscience take that child away from the only person who has remained a constant in her young life?"

Lucie groaned. "Yeah, I see the problem."

Kate heard another phone ringing and quickly realized that it was her cell phone, which she'd left in the bedroom. "Lucie, my cell phone is ringing. Hold on, will you?"

"Sure."

Kate laid the phone down on the desk, ran into the bedroom and grabbed her cell phone up off the bedside table. She flipped it open.

"Kate Malone."

"Kate, it's Dante Moran."

Kate gasped, her breath caught in her throat.

"The DNA test results just arrived."

"And?"

"Christa Farrell is your and Trent's child."

"Oh, my God!" Tears clouded Kate's vision. Her heart swelled with happiness.

"Would you like for me to try to set up a meeting for you and Trent to meet with Christa's grandmother, Brenda Farrell?"

"Yes, yes. Please. Tell her we'll do whatever she wants, handle it anyway she wants to, just as long as she'll meet with us and give us a chance to—" Kate's voice cracked.

"Go tell Trent the good news," Moran said. "I'll get back in touch with you when I work something out with Mrs. Farrell."

"Thank you. Thank you so much."

"Kate?"

"Huh?"

"Don't expect too much."

"Yeah, I know. I'll try not to, but…oh, mercy. Mary Kate is alive. And I—I saw her. She's—damn, Moran, I shouldn't have admitted that to you."

Moran chuckled. "It's okay. Don't you think I knew you'd find those addresses?"

"Yeah, I halfway figured out that you'd left them where I could find them."

"I've got to run, but I'll talk to you again very soon."

"Bye."

Kate closed her cell phone, then flew into the lounge and picked up the telephone receiver from the desk. "Lucie! That was Moran. I was right. The DNA test proved that Christa Farrell is Mary Kate."

"Wow! That's great, hon."

"Moran will try to set up a meeting with Christa's grandmother. Keep your fingers crossed for us."

"So how's Trent taking the news?'

"Oh, Lord, he doesn't know. He's not here. I've got to hang up now, Lucie, and call him."

"Keep me posted. And good luck."

"Thanks. Bye."

Hurriedly Kate dialed Trent's cell phone number. He answered on the fifth ring.

"Trent, come back to the hotel immediately," Kate told him.

"What's wrong?"

"Nothing's wrong. Moran just called. The DNA test results are back."

"And?"

"And Christa Farrell is Mary Kate."

Brenda Farrell's home, situated in an area of Sheffield known as the Village, was a neat cream stucco with rust-red shutters and a red-tile roof. Large old trees graced the lawn and neat shrubbery lined the brick walkway leading from the street to the fancy wood and glass front door.

Trent pulled the Bentley into the driveway at the side of the house, then got out and hurried to open the passenger door. Kate couldn't remember ever being so nervous. She'd had to ask Trent to stop twice on the drive from Memphis because she'd been sick to her stomach. Ever since yesterday when Dante Moran had phoned her with the good news, that Mrs. Farrell had reluctantly agreed to meet with them, Kate had been a bundle of nerves.

"Are you okay?" Trent asked, a worried frown wrinkling his forehead.

Kate nodded nervously and offered him a frail smile. "I want this meeting to go well. I'm so thankful Dante was able to persuade Mrs. Farrell to see us. I want her to like us." She grasped Trent's hand. "Oh, Trent, I don't know if I can bear it if anything goes wrong."

"Nothing is going to go wrong." He squeezed her hand. "But we can't expect too much too soon. Mrs. Farrell agreeing to allow us to meet Christa today is more than I expected."

"You're right. I never dreamed she'd be so generous."

Trent put his arm around Kate's shoulders and hugged her. "Come on. Take a deep breath. We're going to meet our daughter."

Kate took that deep breath as she and Trent headed toward the front entrance. Before they had a chance to ring the bell, the door opened. A petite, plump woman with short salt-and-pepper hair and striking blue eyes inspected them from head to toe, then smiled uneasily.

"You must be Kate and Trent," she said in a soft Southern drawl. "Please, won't y'all come in. I'm Christa's nana, Brenda Farrell." She stepped aside and swept her hand through the air in a gracious, inviting gesture.

Trent nudged Kate into action. They went inside, into a sunroom-type foyer filled with a variety of green plants.

"Thank you for seeing us so soon, Mrs. Farrell," Trent said.

"Yes, we appreciate this so much," Kate added.

"Come on into the living room. I've put on coffee and I can fix hot tea, if you'd like."

They followed her into the neat, country-style living room, filled with large comfy-looking chairs, an over-stuffed sofa and an oak armoire used as an entertainment center.

"Please, don't go to any trouble," Kate said.

"Take off your coats and sit down." Brenda motioned with her hand. "Christa isn't here. She's next door with our neighbors, the Kimbroughs."

Kate and Trent removed their coats, laid them across the arm of a nearby chair, and then sat side by side on the sofa. Brenda remained standing.

"We understood from Special Agent Moran that we might get to meet Christa today," Trent said.

"I thought it best for the three of us to talk first, then if…" Brenda cleared her throat. "You must realize that I've been devastated by this whole thing. Learning that Christa was stolen from her birth parents, that she wasn't willingly given up for adoption. I'm simply brokenhearted. For both of you and for me. But mostly for Christa. That sweet child hasn't fully recovered from losing her parents—my son Rick and his wife Jean. I can't bear the thought of her suffering more than she already has."

"Please believe us, Mrs. Farrell, the last thing we want to do is hurt Christa in any way." Kate's voice quavered every so slightly. "She's our daughter, our little Mary Kate. We want only what's best for her."

Trent grabbed Kate's hand and held it tightly. "Mrs. Farrell, we're not here to demand our parental rights. And we're not here to take Christa away from you. First and foremost, we want our child—your granddaughter—to be happy and well and safe."

Tears glimmered in Brenda Farrell's azure blue eyes. "Call me Brenda."

"Brenda, we're so grateful to your son and his wife and to you for taking such good care of Mary—of Christa," Kate said. "All these years, we didn't know where our daughter was or what had happened to her. We're so thankful she's all right."

"Christa is a dear child and I love her more than anything on earth. She's all I have. My son was an only child and—" Brenda sucked in her breath and released it through clenched teeth. "When Rick and Jean died, I brought Christa to live with me. She had terrible nightmares every night for months on end. I saw to it that she got professional help and eventually the nightmares went away. For the most part. Occasionally, when she's under stress, she still has a terrible dream. But basically she's mentally healthy."

"I'm sure we owe you so much," Kate said.

Brenda glanced away. "Let me get that coffee now. How do y'all take it?"

"Black," Trent replied.

"May I help you?" Kate asked.

"No, please, I need a few minutes alone. I'll prepare the coffee and afterward, I'll call next door and asked Edna to send Christa home."

Trent and Kate exchanged hopeful glances, but neither spoke. Brenda walked out of the living room and into the dining room. She paused at the swinging door leading into the kitchen. With her back still to them, she said, "I've told Christa about y'all. She knows she's going to meet her biological parents today."

Kate came halfway up off the sofa before Trent grabbed her and dragged her back down. When she glared at him, he shook his head. Brenda Farrell disappeared into the kitchen.

"She told Christa about us." Kate planted her hands on Trent's chest. "What if she didn't explain everything? What if Christa thinks we gave her away? No, dammit, no, Trent, I won't have my child believing I willingly gave her up."

Trent laid his hands over hers and pulled them down from his chest. "Stay calm, honey. We don't know what Mrs. Farrell…Brenda…told Christa. But I'm sure whatever she told her, she didn't say anything negative about us. Stop and think, will you? Brenda seems to be a very intelligent lady. She wouldn't do something that might antagonize us anymore than we'd do something to antagonize her. We're all in the same boat here. She wants to protect Christa and so do we. We all love her."

Realizing she was on the edge, tilting precariously close to diving headfirst into calamity, Kate willed herself under control. She reminded herself that Trent was right. Christa's grandmother was hardly likely to do anything that would harm the child.

The child? God, Kate, the child is Mary Kate. Your little Mary Kate.

Fidgety and partially nauseated because she'd been unable to eat a bite since breakfast, Kate rose from the sofa and moved around the living room. Pictures on the mantel caught her eye immediately. She moved closer to get a better look. Her mouth opened on a silent gasp when she realized the line of frames adorning the mantel were filled with photographs of Christa at various ages. Several showed her with a couple Kate assumed were Rick and Jean Farrell. One picture in particular drew Kate's attention. A baby picture of Christa. And from the decorative background and the red velvet dress she wore, Kate figured it was Christa's first Christmas. Big brown eyes sparkled. A small red velvet bow nested in her golden blond curls. This was the child Kate remembered, the child she'd carried in her heart for nearly twelve years.

Trent came up behind her and wrapped his arms around her, then nuzzled the side of her face. "It's going to be all right," he whispered. "Somehow, someway, we'll make it all right. We'll see it through together this time."

Kate clutched Trent's arms that held her and snuggled backward into his embrace. "Do you think there's a solution that will work for everyone involved? Is it possible that Brenda Farrell would be willing to—"

"Coffee." Brenda returned to the living room, a small serving tray in her hands.

Kate and Trent accepted the cups of coffee and returned to the sofa. Brenda placed the tray on the dining room table, then lifted her cup and came back into the living room. She sat across from them in a large, floral wing chair.

"I know that as Christa's biological parents, you two have certain legal rights," Brenda said, gripping her cup in a shaky hand. "But I'm counting on y'all being good people who won't take Christa away from me. It would destroy her if she lost me. We're very close."

"We have no intention of taking Christa away from you," Trent assured her. "If her adoptive parents were still alive, we'd ask only to see Christa and over the years maintain contact so that when she became an adult she could chose whether she wanted to get to know us. But since your son and his wife died six years ago, leaving Christa without parents, I'd like for us to find a way where we can share Christa."

"Share her?" Brenda set her cup on a coaster atop the coffee table. "I don't understand. Are you suggesting an arrangement where she lives with you two part of the time and me part of the time? I was told you two are divorced. Is that right?"

"What I'm suggesting is that you and Christa come to Prospect for a visit," Trent said. "I have a large home with more than enough room for all of us. And yes, Kate and I are divorced, but at least for the initial visit, I'm sure Kate would be perfectly willing to stay in Prospect and live at Winston Hall with us."

Kate sipped on the coffee, hoping it wouldn't hit her stomach like a lead weight. Why hadn't Trent mentioned his great idea to her—his plans to bring Christa and her grandmother to Prospect?

"How long a visit are we talking about?" Brenda inquired.

"That would be up to you. I suggest at least a week the first time."

"I see. Well, I suppose it's something I can consider."

"You don't need to decide tonight," Trent told her. "Take a few days. Talk it over with Christa. You have the opportunity to give her a mother and a father, as well as a great aunt. And you and she wouldn't lose each other. If things worked out, you might consider moving to Prospect."

Wait just a damn minute, Kate wanted to shout. *What about me? I live in Atlanta. Am I suppose to visit Prospect when I want to see my child?*

"I'll think seriously about a visit…soon." Brenda rose from the chair. "I'll go get Christa. Please, remember that y'all are strangers to her. Don't expect her to be happy to see you."

"We understand." Trent looked at Kate. "Don't we, honey?"

Kate nodded.

The minute Brenda left, Kate turned on Trent. "When did you come up with your brilliant idea for Brenda and Christa to visit Winston Hall?"

"You're angry. Why?"

"Why? Because you took charge, made decisions about our child's future without so much as mentioning anything to me. You could have—no!—you should have discussed this with me before you—"

"Hell, Kate, the idea just hit me while we were sitting here. I thought you'd be thrilled if I could get Brenda to agree to bring Christa to Prospect for a week. It would give us a chance to get to know her and for her to get to know her family."

"And what family would that be? You and Aunt Mary Belle and a legion of Winston cousins?"

Trent shot to his feet and stomped around the room, grumbling under his breath. After several minutes of letting off steam, he stopped and looked right at Kate. "Get this through your head right now, so there won't be any misunderstandings later—you and I were Mary Kate's parents so that means you and I are Christa's parents. She's ours. Not mine. Not yours. Ours."

Her nerves raw, her emotions barely kept in check, Kate shivered. "Ours," she said hoarsely.

"If Brenda agrees, she'll bring Christa to Winston Hall for a visit with you and me. And yes, with Aunt Mary Belle, too. We'll spend time together, getting acquainted. Later on, we might try a two-week or even monthlong visit. Or it could be that things will work out so well the first visit that we can make it a permanent arrangement."

"What about me? About my job? My life in Atlanta?"

Trent's expression hardened. "I had thought you'd..." He cleared his throat. "If you don't want to come home to Prospect on a permanent basis, then I could bring Mary Kate—I mean Christa—to Atlanta. Or if you prefer, Brenda could bring her to see you."

The kitchen door opened. Brenda walked in, Christa beside her, clutching Brenda's hand. Kate felt as if her heart stopped, as if the whole world had stopped, as she and Trent turned to meet their daughter.

"Christa, this is Kate and Trent. They're the people I told you about. Your birth parents."

Zeroing in on Kate first and then Trent, the child studied them closely. "You're the man and woman I saw at the library the other day."

"What?" Brenda gasped.

"We came to Sheffield to take a look at Christa," Trent said. "We couldn't wait to see her and we also went by Corinth to see another little girl who might have been our Mary Kate."

"I was the one who couldn't wait," Kate admitted. "I was so anxious to find out if…I wanted Christa to be my daughter."

"I'm not your daughter," Christa said. "Rick and Jean Farrell were my parents. I belong to Nana now. She and I have each other and we don't need anyone else, do we, Nana?" Christa looked pleadingly at her grandmother.

"We'll always have each other." Brenda put her arm around Christa and hugged her close. "Kate and Trent aren't here to take you away from me. I told you they're just here to meet you." When Christa buried her face against her grandmother's chest, Brenda stroked her back lovingly.

"Where are your manners, Christa?" Brenda eased her granddaughter away from her and turned her to face their company. "Say hello to Kate and Trent, then go sit down and we'll have a nice visit."

Tears swimming in her chocolate brown eyes—eyes identical to her father's—Christa glared at her parents. Kate felt as if her heart would break in two. Here was her baby girl, her precious Mary Kate, and the child wanted nothing to do with her.

"Hello," Christa said, her voice a mere whisper.

"Hello," Trent replied.

Christa glanced at Kate, who managed a wavering smile.

"Hello, Christa. I'm so very glad to meet you."

"Why don't you tell Kate and Trent about school," Brenda said. "Tell them what grade you're in and who your teacher is and—"

"No! I won't tell them anything." Christa burst into tears. "Go away. Both of you. I don't know you. You aren't my parents. I'll never leave my nana. Not ever!" Christa ran out of the room.

"Oh, dear." Brenda clasped her hand over her mouth.

"Shouldn't you go after her?" Kate asked, wanting nothing more than to rush after Christa and wrap the child in her arms.

Brenda sighed. "No. When she throws one of her temper tantrums, I've found it best to leave her alone for a while until she calms down."

"That's exactly the way Aunt Mary Belle handled me when I acted like that," Trent said.

Brenda faced them. "I'm so sorry. I thought I had prepared her for this meeting. Apparently I didn't do such a good job."

"It's not your fault," Kate told her. "It's not anyone's fault."

"I think we'd better go." Trent placed his hand beneath Kate's elbow. "We'll stay in town overnight, so if you think it's all right, Kate and I will come back tomorrow."

"I have your cell phone number." Brenda came over and put her hand on Kate's shoulder. "I can only imagine what you must be feeling right now. I am so sorry, my dear."

"Maybe she'll be willing to see us tomorrow." Kate clenched her teeth to keep herself from crying.

She turned and all but ran through the sunroom and out the front door. She was almost to the Bentley when Trent caught up with her. He whirled her around and pulled her into his arms. She melted against him. And cried.

Ten

Trent had gotten them a suite at the Holiday Inn, which was the best Sheffield, Alabama, had to offer. She doubted the employees had ever catered to a guest who drove a Bentley. And from the fact that the manager himself escorted them to their suite, Kate figured the entire staff was duly impressed with Trenton Bayard Winston IV. Odd how most people admired and respected money in a way they did little else.

While the manager kowtowed to Trent, Kate went into the bathroom to escape. She had cried almost the whole way from the Village to the hotel and she now had a killer headache. She turned on the sink faucets, cupped her hands to catch the water and splashed her face, then grabbed a hand towel from the nearby stack and patted her skin dry. Sighing, she flipped the commode lid closed and slumped down on the seat. She felt like a balloon with all the air let out, deflated by a slow, painful leak that had left her flat and lifeless.

Mary Kate wanted nothing to do with them.

No, not Mary Kate—Christa.

She had to get the fact straight in her mind that although Mary Kate was Christa, Christa was not Mary Kate. The baby she and Trent had brought into this world, nurtured and loved for over two months, no longer existed. That child had ceased to exist the day she'd been stolen from Kate. Christa Farrell had no memories of her previous life, no emotional connection to Trent and Kate. They were, as Brenda had pointed out to them, strangers to their own child.

What were they going to do? What if Christa never came around? What if she never wanted them to be a part of her life? *Oh, God, how will I be able to bear it?* Kate's heart wept. Bowing her head, she covered her face with her hands and moaned, the grief welling up inside her, ripping her apart in its wake.

The bathroom door opened. She glanced up to see Trent enter. He came to her, knelt in front of her and clasped her hands, completely covering them with his. She looked at him and saw her own pain reflected in his eyes.

"Oh, Trent…"

"Let it go, honey. Rant and rave and cry some more, if that's what you need to do."

She shook her head. "What good will that do? Besides, I'm not the ranting and raving type. And I've already cried an ocean of tears."

"Yeah, I'm the one with the temper. Believe me, I really need about an hour working out at the gym, preferably with a punching bag."

Kate reached out and caressed his face. "What are we going to do?"

"We're going to wait until tomorrow and hope that Christa will be willing to see us then." Trent took Kate's hands and urged her to stand, which she did. "But for tonight, we're going to try to put today's events behind us. I've arranged for room service, so our dinner should be here within the hour. In the meantime, I'll draw you a warm bath and you can soak in the tub while I make a few phone calls."

"Who are you going to call?"

"Aunt Mary Belle, Dante Moran and my lawyer. I've got the name of a top man in the field of child custody cases. I want to put him on a retainer."

Kate nodded. She didn't know for sure why he would call Moran, but she didn't really care. Not at this precise moment. And as for hiring a lawyer, she'd leave that up to Trent. At least for now. "A warm bath sounds good. I'll get my pajamas and robe—"

"You aren't going to do anything except relax and allow me to take care of you." He went over and turned on the faucets, then unwrapped the guest soap and laid it atop a washcloth on the edge of the tub. After that he set the small bottles of shampoo and conditioner alongside the cloth. "Undress and get in. I'll bring your robe and slippers in here shortly."

"Thank you."

"My pleasure."

As soon as he exited the bathroom, Kate removed her clothes and stepped into the tub. She slid down into the delicious warm water and sighed with contentment. The water level rose higher and higher and when it covered her almost to her neck, she turned off the faucets and laid her head against the back of the tub. She rested in that position for a good five minutes, doing her best to clear her mind of all unpleasant thoughts. Her headache didn't go away, but the throbbing eased up considerably. She soaped the washcloth and scrubbed herself from face to feet. After shampooing, rinsing, conditioning and rinsing again, she let out some of the cooling water and refilled with fresh warm water.

She stayed in the tub for quite some time, soaking away the stress of the day and her body's minor aches and pains. Not until Trent entered the bathroom again did she realize she'd practically dosed off. Glancing up at him, she smiled when she saw he held a small glass in his hands.

"That looks like wine," she said.

"It is wine." Trent grinned. "Compliments of the manager."

"How long have I been in here?" she asked. "I seem to have lost track of time."

"About twenty minutes." He walked over to the tub and held the glass out to her.

She didn't feel the least bit awkward being naked in front of Trent. She supposed she should, but she didn't. He had been her first lover, her husband for more than two years and he had once known every inch of her body better than she had.

Kate took the glass from him, sipped the wine and sighed. "Not bad."

"Finish that off while I get your robe and slippers."

She sipped the red wine, savoring the taste and appreciating its ability, if she drank enough, to partially anesthesize her. Just as she finished drinking the wine, Trent returned carrying her robe. He hung it on the back of the door, then snapped open a large towel and came toward the tub. She understood that he was holding it for her, waiting to wrap her in it when she emerged from her watery bed.

If you allow him to take care of you, things can and probably will get out of control, she told herself. *Is that what you want?*

Kate set the empty glass in the floor, then rose from the water and stepped out of the tub and right into Trent's waiting arms. He wrapped the towel around her and led her over to the commode, the lid still down. After seating her, he took another towel and rubbed her hair until all the excess moisture was absorbed. Using another towel, he dried her feet and calves, dropped that towel to the floor, and then opened the towel draped around her and gently patted her stomach, breasts and neck. Kate drew in a quivering breath.

"You're even more beautiful now than you were when we first got married." He whipped the towel off her and gazed appreciatively at her body.

Her nipples peaked. "You're a skillful liar," she told him. "And I thank you. I suppose I'm in pretty good shape to be thirty-five, but—"

He placed his index finger over her lips to silence her. "You're in great shape." He reached out tentatively, bringing the tips of his fingers to one breast.

She sucked in her breath. He grazed the nipple softly.

"You can't imagine how much I want you," he admitted, his gaze hungry as it moved from her breasts, down her belly to the downy apex between her thighs.

"Maybe I can," she told him, "if it's half as much as I want you."

"Kate?"

"A little comfort to soothe our battle scars?" she asked.

"Label it whatever suits you. Comfort. Lust. Mutual need."

She leaned forward, placed her hands on his cheeks

and cupped his face. "Just for tonight." She wouldn't ask him for any promises, wouldn't expect a commitment just because they had sex again.

"Yeah, honey, just for tonight."

He lifted her up and into his arms. She cuddled close as he carried her from the bathroom to the bedroom. After laying her on the turned-down bed, he stripped out of his clothes. She expected him to join her, but instead he went back in the bathroom. Within seconds he returned, a small bottle of lotion in his hand.

"Roll over," he told her.

Without questioning him, she did as he'd asked. He sat on the bed, screwed off the bottle lid and poured lotion into his hand, then he spread the cool, lightly scented cream across her back and shoulders. She relaxed as he massaged and caressed her. He worked his way down each arm, then along her spine and over her buttocks. A tingling sensation spread through her, like minuscule currents of electricity bringing her body to life.

Trent rubbed the back of her thighs, her calves and even her feet. When they were married, he'd often given her this type of sensual massage and it always ended with sweet and tender lovemaking. The kind of lovemaking that lingered in the body and on the mind for hours afterward.

"Turn over," he said, his voice husky with desire.

She turned slowly, languidly, an odd combination of relaxation and excitement controlling her movements. Her breasts felt heavy and achy. Her nipples were spiked points, begging for attention. Her femininity clutched and released, creating tension between her legs. Moisture gathered between her intimate lips and sexual heat warmed her from head to toe.

Trent used what little was left of the lotion on Kate's belly and hips, his big hands amazingly gentle as they stroked her flesh. When she thought she couldn't bear his ardent attention another minute, he came down over her, his erection pressing against her stomach.

His mouth covered hers and they shared a long, lingering kiss. His lips moved across her cheek to moisten her earlobe. "I want to be inside you. Deep." He licked a path down her neck, then lifted his head and looked right into her eyes. "I want to take you and take you and take you." He flicked the tip of his tongue over one pouting nipple and then the other, eliciting a cry of pleasure-pain from her lips. "Once isn't going to be enough."

She gave herself over to the moment, to Trent and to the love that had never died. While he suckled her breasts, she ran her hands over his broad shoulders and across his back, loving the feel of him. His sex throbbed against her, arousing her even more.

"Trent, please…"

"Not yet, honey."

His hands, lips and tongue explored her body, each little nook and cranny, turning every inch of her into a quivering mass of sexual need. Just when she thought he was going to enter her, he withdrew from her and leaned over to pick up something off the nightstand.

She whimpered.

"I had the hotel manager send out for some condoms," Trent said, a wicked grin on his face.

"You didn't?" Kate giggled.

"I did."

"What must he think?"

"Who cares? But he probably thinks that I wanted to make love to my wife."

"Your wife?"

"That's how I registered. Mr. and Mrs. Winston."

The former Mrs. Winston sighed, then held open her arms, issuing Mr. Winston an invitation.

Hurriedly he undid the foil packet, sheathed his sex and returned to her. When he slid his hands beneath her hips and lifted her up, she wrapped her arms around his neck. He slipped into her with one slick, even stroke. And she was in heaven. Back in Trent's arms. Their bodies intimately joined. Their loving was as natural as breathing to each of them, as if they had been created for only each other. They kissed and touched without rushing, no urgency fueling their desire. She sensed that he was being intentionally gentle, drawing out each precious moment, making it last as long as possible. He did all the giving, showering her with attention.

Kate had never felt so cherished, so completely adored, as she did tonight. Trent's every touch, every move, every word was a form of worship. After he had brought her near fulfillment several times, then held back to intensify her satisfaction, he finally allowed her to do more than enjoy the pleasure he gave her. Their loving became a mutual giving and taking, the passion growing stronger and hotter by the moment. As her body tightened, the end close, Trent quickened the pace, pumping into her hard and fast.

This was right. This was so right.

Her climax hit her with the force of an explosion. Although he was buried deep inside her, hammering her repeatedly, she bucked up, seeking to gain the last ounce of release. And just as the waves of completion washed over her, Trent groaned. He came with a fury, his hard, hot body trembling with fulfillment.

I love you. The words were on the tip of her tongue.

It would be the most natural thing in the world to tell him how she felt. But she couldn't. Not unless he said the words first.

When he rolled off onto his back, she snuggled against him. He shoved his arm beneath her and hugged her to his side, then he stroked her naked hip. The aftershocks of her climax rippled through her as she kissed his chest.

"God, Kate, I've missed you."

And she had missed him, more than she'd realized. "It was always so good…so right with us, wasn't it?"

He kissed her temple. "Always."

She lay there in the semidarkness of their hotel suite, waiting for him to say those three magic words. Moments ticked by. Neither of them spoke again until a loud knock on the door roused them.

"Room service," a feminine voice called.

"Damn! I'd forgotten about ordering supper." Trent jumped out of bed. "Be there in a minute," he yelled. He found his slacks on the floor, picked them up and rushed into the bathroom. When he reentered the bedroom, he grinned at Kate. "You stay right there. I'll go to the door and bring the serving cart in myself."

By the time Trent wheeled in their evening meal, Kate had slipped on her house shoes and robe. Despite the fact that her ex-husband had not mentioned love before, during or after their lovemaking, Kate appreciated the efforts he'd gone to for her sake.

"Dinner is served," Trent said.

"Good. I'm starving."

"Save room for dessert," he told her and winked.

"Don't tell me—whipped cream and strawberries?" They had indulged in those items during their honeymoon, putting more of the cream on each other than on the berries.

"No strawberries," he said, then lifted the cover from a large, round bowl. "But lots of whipped cream."

Kate laughed. Only Trent could have worked this miracle. Only Trent could have taken her mind off their problems and given her such pleasure.

Trent's cell phone rang at eight o'clock the next morning, just as Kate and he were dressing after the shower they'd taken together. They had made love again the night before, using the whipped cream to full advantage. And then he'd awakened her before six this morning and they'd made love for a third time. He couldn't get enough of her. But that wasn't something new. It had always been that way with them. The passion had never faded, even when the love and trust had wavered.

How could he have ever let her leave him? Why hadn't he done more to save their marriage? Hurt pride and his own feelings of guilt had paralyzed him when she'd asked him for a divorce. Kate had been the best thing that ever happened to him, but he hadn't been able to hold on to her after they'd lost their child.

Wearing only a towel around his waist, Trent came out of the bathroom and removed his cell phone from his coat pocket. He flipped it open and said hello.

"Trent, this is Brenda Farrell." His heartbeat accelerated.

"Yes, Brenda, how are you this morning?"

"I'm all right, considering the fact that I slept very little last night." She paused and when Trent didn't say anything, she continued. "I've done a great deal of thinking and soul searching and I've decided that the best thing for Christa is to get to know you and Kate. She deserves to have two loving parents again and I'd be selfish to keep y'all away from each other."

Kate came up to Trent and draped her arm around his waist, then mouthed the question, "Who is it?"

"You can't imagine how glad I am to hear you say that, Brenda." He emphasized her name for Kate's benefit.

"Brenda." Kate whispered the name.

Trent nodded. Kate stood on tiptoes and dragged Trent down enough so that she could put her ear against the phone in order to hear the telephone conversation.

"Christa isn't being cooperative," Brenda said. "I need some time to bring her around. I don't think it's a good idea for y'all to see her today."

Trent's heart sank. "How much time do you need?"

"Just until her birthday. That's not long."

"Mary Kate's birthday is February the fourth."

"We've always celebrated Christa's birthday on the seventh. That's the date on her birth certificate, the one the adoption agency provided Rick and Jean."

"Are you saying we can see Christa again on February seventh?"

"I'm saying that I want to bring Christa to Prospect the day before her birthday for a weeklong stay with you and Kate. I'll make arrangements with her school so that she can make up any work she misses. And you do understand that I'll want to stay with her in Prospect. I can't leave her there. She would feel totally abandoned."

"Of course, you'll come with her," Trent said. "And we'll have a birthday party for Christa, if that's all right with you."

"Yes, that would be very nice. I'd thought perhaps y'all would enjoy giving her a small party."

"We'd love it. Thank you for doing this."

"I realize it won't be easy for you and Kate to wait for a while longer, but please, trust me. I want what's best for my granddaughter and if we can all be a part of her life, then no one has to lose, most of all Christa. If we can work things out to everyone's satisfaction, Christa will be the real winner."

"I agree completely."

"I'll contact you again later on to get driving directions and—"

"I can send someone to get you and Christa, if you'd like."

"Thank you, but that won't be necessary."

"All right. Whatever you want."

"If you'd like to call me to check on Christa, I won't mind. Tell Kate she can call me everyday if she wants to."

"I'll tell her. We appreciate the way you're handling this situation."

"I don't want any of us to suffer more than we already have."

"We feel the same."

"Goodbye, Trent."

The phone went dead. Brenda had hung up. He tossed the phone into a nearby chair, turned and lifted Kate off her feet.

"Brenda is bringing Christa to Prospect to spend a week with us, beginning on the sixth of February."

Trent swung Kate around and around, then stopped and slid her down his body, effectively knocking the towel from his hips. He pulled her into his arms and kissed her soundly.

"You and I are going to give our daughter a birthday party for her twelfth birthday."

"Oh, Trent, this is too good to be true."

"It's true, honey. It's true."

He kissed her again and before either of them knew what was happening, they were back in bed and making love again.

Eleven

Kate arrived at Winston Hall around twelve-thirty on the sixth of February. Guthrie met her at the door, welcomed her home and told her that Mr. Trent was in court until three o'clock this afternoon and Miss Mary Belle, who was having lunch in the breakfast room, would be delighted if Kate joined her. She sucked it up, stiffened her spine and marched into the lion's den. To her great surprise, Kate was met with open arms and a warm smile. Mary Belle hugged her with great affection, then took her hand and led her to the table where two places had been set for the noon meal.

"The minute you telephoned to let us know you'd be here by lunchtime, I had Cook prepare salmon croquettes," Mary Belle said. "As I recall, they were one of your favorites."

"Yes, thank you."

Kate sat down across from Mary Belle, in a semi-state of shock. Cook brought in their salads first and smiled at Kate. "Good to have you back, Miss Kate."

"Iced tea—no sugar," Mary Belle said. "That is right, isn't it? And we'll have our Earl Grey with dessert. A delicious raspberry torte."

"Miss Mary Belle, you've gone to a great deal of trouble just for me," Kate said. "I'm not sure I understand why."

"It's Aunt Mary Belle. You're family, dear girl. And seeing that you have a nice lunch was no trouble at all. As to not understanding my motives for being nice to you—I'd think that would be apparent. I very much want to make it up to you for anything I did wrong in the past. I never meant to hurt you or add to the problems you and Trent were having after Mary Kate was kidnapped. I am sorry. Genuinely sorry."

Kate stared at Trent's aunt. A funny thought crossed her mind. Who was this woman and what had happened to the real Mary Belle Winston?

"You're speechless." Mary Belle laughed. "I love Trent more than anyone on earth and his happiness means everything to me. When he returned to Prospect a couple of weeks ago, he was happier than I've ever seen him since you two divorced. All he's talked about is that Kate and Christa were coming to Prospect to spend a week with us."

"Trent and I are eager to see our daughter again and we're praying that we say and do all the right things. I'm sure Trent told you that our first meeting with her didn't turn out very well." After their night together at the Holiday Inn in Sheffield, Kate had flown back to Atlanta to put her house in order, so to speak, and Trent had returned to Prospect to his job as a circuit court judge. During this period of waiting, they had spoken on the phone almost every day. They had been preparing for the upcoming week when Christa and her nana would stay at Winston Hall for seven whole days.

"I understand completely and I, too, want to do all I can to make sure nothing goes wrong." Mary Belle looked at Kate beseechingly. "I've made some arrangements that I want to discuss with you. And if there's anything you want changed, anything you disapprove of, just let me know and we'll—"

"Aunt Mary Belle, have you actually changed so much that I hardly recognize you, or did I not ever really know you?"

Mary Belle's eyes widened. "Perhaps a bit of both. I'd like to think that I'm not only older, but wiser. And in the past, I spent so much time trying to tutor you, to help you adjust to being a Winston, that I didn't let you know how terribly fond of you I was."

"You were fond of me? I thought you disliked me, that you disapproved of me, that you thought I was unworthy of being Trent's wife."

Mary Belle frowned, deepening the faint wrinkles around her mouth and eyes. "It's true that at first, I had certain reservations. You weren't one of us and...forgive me. You know what a snob I can be. I simply can't help it." She laughed nervously. "But it didn't take me long to see what a good person you were and to realize how much you and Trent loved each other. I suppose I tried too hard to make you over into what I thought Trent's wife should be. But I assure you, I believed I was doing the right thing, for Trent and for you."

"And what about now? I'm not Trent's wife any longer."

"You should be and we both know it. He's never

gotten over you and I suspect you're still in love with him, too, aren't you?"

"How much does your solicitous attitude have to do with Christa Farrell?"

"I won't deny that I hope you and Trent will remarry and make a home for Mary Kate. Yes, yes, I know. I'll have to make myself call her Christa."

Kate sighed. For once she and Aunt Mary Belle wanted exactly the same thing. "Don't forget that Christa has a grandmother who has raised her single-handedly since she was six."

"Winston Hall is a large house," Mary Belle said. "There is room for all of us, including Brenda Farrell."

"You'd be willing to let Brenda live here, too?"

"I'm willing to do whatever it takes to make all of us a family again."

"I see." Kate thought things over for a couple of minutes, then said, "Tell me about the arrangements you've made for Christa and her nana's visit."

Trent arrived home less than ten minutes before Brenda Farrell drove up in her older-model Chevrolet. He'd barely had time to give Kate a hug and a kiss, discard his briefcase and ask her how her trip from Atlanta had gone before their much anticipated guests arrived.

With Trent, Kate and Mary Belle lined up in the foyer, Guthrie opened the door and invited their visitors to come inside. Brenda all but shoved a reluctant Christa over the threshold. Both grandmother and child gawked at the massive foyer, the winding staircase, the impressive grandeur of the old family home. Christa clung to her grandmother's hand, an expression of uncertainty on her face.

"Welcome to Winston Hall," Trent said. "I hope y'all had a pleasant trip down from Sheffield."

"Very pleasant," Brenda replied. "Christa, don't you have something to say to Trent and Kate?"

Kate sought and found Trent's hand, then squeezed tightly. He suspected she was as nervous as he and needed moral support, just as he did.

"Thank you very much for inviting us for a visit," Christa said, but there was little sincerity in her words.

"You're quite welcome," Trent replied. "Would y'all care for some refreshments?"

"No, thank you," Christa said.

"Perhaps you'd like for your mother—for Kate to show you up to your room," Mary Belle suggested, a slight quiver to her voice and tears misting her eyes.

Christa stared at Mary Belle.

"I'm your great-aunt Mary Belle. I was born in this house and have lived here all my life. This is your home, too, you know. You lived here with us for the first two months of your life and we all loved you very much."

"I don't remember," Christa said. "Nana has told me that my birth mother didn't give me away." She looked right at Kate. "Somebody stole me from you, didn't they?"

Kate nodded. Tears glistened in her eyes. When she opened her mouth, but no sound came out, Trent realized she was too overcome with emotion to speak.

"Kate and I loved you so," Trent said. "You were our precious little Mary Kate. You were the joy of our lives."

"I'm not Mary Kate anymore. I'm sorry your baby was stolen and I'm sorry I don't remember either of you." She glanced at Mary Belle. "Or you."

"It's all right, Christa," Kate said. "It doesn't matter. All that matters is that you're here for a visit and we're going to get to know each other all over again."

"Nana told me that y'all have promised you won't take me away from her."

"No, we will never take you away from your grandmother," Kate vowed. "Isn't that right, Trent?"

"That's right. We want your nana to be a part of our family, too."

Christa's expression changed instantly, all wariness disappeared, replaced with curiosity. "I've never seen a house this big. It's very old, isn't it?"

"Yes, it's very old," Mary Belle said. "Would you like for Trent and Kate to give you a grand tour while your grandmother and I have tea in the parlor so she and I can become better acquainted?"

"Is that all right, Nana?"

"Certainly," Brenda said.

"What would you like to see first?" Trent gave Kate's hand a it's-going-to-be-all-right squeeze.

"I don't know." Christa thought for a couple of minutes. "Did I have a room of my own when I lived here?"

"You had a beautiful nursery," Kate said.

"I don't guess it's still a nursery, is it?"

Kate looked to Trent for an answer. When she'd left Winston Hall over ten years ago, Mary Kate's nursery had been untouched, looking just as it had that Easter Sunday when she'd been abducted.

"Your nursery is just as it was," Trent said. "But Aunt Mary Belle had a new, larger room decorated just for you—for twelve-year-old Christa Farrell."

"Really?"

"Really," Trent said.

"May I see both—my old nursery and my new room?"

"You most certainly may."

Trent held his hand out to his daughter. She accepted without hesitation and went with him up the long, winding staircase, Kate keeping in step on Christa's other side.

* * *

Kate now wished she had listened to her gut instincts and insisted that Aunt Mary Belle pare down the extravagant birthday party she'd planned for Christa. But she'd told herself she was being silly to think that just because all the Winston hoopla had scared the bejesus out of her when she'd been dating Trent, Christa would be overwhelmed by a guest list of fifty, a live band, a clown, a magician, hot-and-cold running servants, a birthday cake five feet high and a pile of presents that could have been for ten little girls instead of just one.

Trent walked up beside Kate and whispered, "I'm not sure the Queen of England has parties this elaborate. Do you think maybe Aunt Mary Belle over-did it just a tad?"

"You think?" Kate uttered a nervous chuckle. "Oh, Trent, look at Christa's face. She's out of her league, just the way I always was."

Trent put his arm around Kate's shoulders. "She reminds me so much of you. Her mannerisms are so like yours and the way she laughs and that sweet shyness."

"She's trying valiantly to put on a happy face, but she's simply overwhelmed." Kate shook her head sadly.

"Maybe we should rescue her."

"Could we, Trent? Would it be terribly rude if we got her out of this mausoleum and away from this three-ring circus?"

"To hell with being rude. Let Aunt Mary Belle explain to all these children and their mothers why Christa's parents stole her away before the party was over."

"How do we accomplish this?" Kate asked.

"You go get Christa. Ask her if she'd like to take a ride with us and get away for a while. I'll speak to Brenda to get her permission."

"Let's do it."

Kate mowed her way through hordes of children devouring cake, ice cream and countless bakery delights. Christa sat in a chair that looked somewhat like a small throne in the middle of the room, surrounded by presents, half of which were still gaily wrapped.

Kate leaned down and whispered to her daughter, "Want to get out of here? Trent and I are going for a ride and we thought you might like to go with us."

Christa shot up out of the chair and grabbed Kate's hand. "I'm ready."

Kate led her child from the room, not responding when Aunt Mary Belle called out their names. When they escaped onto the front veranda, Trent followed a moment later and the three of them rushed toward the garage. After hopping inside the front seat of Trent's Bentley, Christa snuggled close to Kate and didn't protest when Kate put her arm around her shoulders. Trent started the engine and backed the car out of the five-car garage, then within minutes they were headed down the road.

"Where are we going?" Christa asked.

"I have something I want to show you and Kate," Trent said. "It's not far from here."

"Is it another birthday surprise?" Christa frowned.

"Not exactly," Trent told her. "It's something for all of us, but especially for Kate."

Christa smiled. "Really?"

"For me?" Kate stared quizzically at Trent.

"Oh, Kate, I forgot to tell Nana that I was going with you and Trent."

"I asked her permission and it's fine with her," Trent said. "She'll be waiting at Winston Hall for us when we return."

Christa's smile widened. "Are you going to give us a hint about what the surprise is?"

"Let's just say that it's something Kate always wanted."

He'd piqued Kate's curiosity by that last statement, but for the life of her she couldn't imagine what it could be. What had she always wanted? All she could think about was Mary Kate, her baby girl. It seemed that being reunited with her child was everything she'd ever wanted.

"Is it bigger than a bread box?" Christa asked.

"Yes," Trent replied.

Joining in the game, Kate asked, "Is it animal, vegetable or mineral?"

Trent laughed. "It's definitely not animal."

"Ah, gee, it's not a horse or a dog or a cat." Christa tapped her index finger on her mouth. "Mmm, hmm, what could it be? You know, I like this guessing game." She turned and looked up at Kate. "Can't you think of anything you always wanted?"

"I always wanted you." The words were out of Kate's mouth before she could stop them.

Christa studied Kate, a curious glint in her brown eyes. "I really am sorry your baby was stolen. I mean, I'm sorry somebody took me away from you. I guess you've missed me a lot, huh? That's what Nana said. She said you and Trent have missed me and want me to be your daughter again."

"Your nana is right," Trent said as he turned onto Third Street. "There's nothing Kate and I want more than a chance to be your parents again."

"You won't expect me to call you Mama and Daddy, will you?"

"No, honey. You can call us anything you'd like. Trent and Kate is just fine with us, isn't it, Kate?"

"Absolutely."

Kate wondered where on earth they were going. She'd thought Trent was taking them into town, but the direction in which they were traveling now took them away from downtown and along the tree-lined streets of the residential section. When Trent turned the corner onto Madison, Kate held her breath. *It can't be. It's just a coincidence that the house I once thought of as my dream home is on Madison.*

"Oh, look, Kate, isn't that a pretty house?" Christa pointed out the old Kirkendall house on the corner at the end of the four-hundred block. She glanced over at Trent. "It's not that Winston Hall isn't beautiful, but it's so big. It doesn't seem like a home at all. It reminds me of a museum."

Trent laughed heartily. "Where have I heard that statement before? Mmm, hmm." He shot Kate a quick glance as he pulled the Bentley into the driveway at the old Kirkendall house. "Your mother—that is Kate—once said the very same thing to me."

Christa bobbed around and looked up at Kate, her lips curved in a big smile. "Did you really tell him that?"

"I sure did." Kate's heart raced wildly.

"We're here," Trent announced. "Let's get out and go inside."

"What?" Kate and Christa cried in unison.

"This is your surprise, Kate."

"I don't understand."

"You mean the house is Kate's surprise?" Christa bounced up and down, all smiles and happy laughter. "You bought Kate a house?"

"Trent, what have you done?"

Christa tugged on Kate's arm. "Come on, let's go see it."

Halfway in a trance, Kate opened the car door and got out, Christa on her heels. Trent rushed around the Bentley's hood and escorted them up the brick walkway to the front porch.

Trent inserted a key in the lock, then opened the front door. "Come on inside."

"This was someone's home," Kate said. "You didn't force some family to move out just so you could give me this house, did you?"

"Christa, see if you can get Kate to come inside and take a look." Trent stepped back to allow them room to enter. "And for your information, Ms. Malone, I bought this house nine years ago, had it completely remodeled at that time and have since completely furnished it."

Christa pulled Kate into the foyer. Shiny wooden floors, polished to a rich gloss spread out from the foyer into the living room and dining room on the left, then went into the paneled den on the right. Kate's mouth dropped open when she saw a glowing fire blazing in the living room fireplace.

Christa danced around and around as she explored the downstairs. "I love this house. It's just perfect. If I come to live with y'all, are we going to live here?"

Trent draped his arm around Kate's shoulders. "What's the answer to that, Kate? Will you come back to Prospect and live in this house with our daughter?"

"Trent…." Tears pooled in Kate's eyes. Not in her wildest dreams had she imagined Trent would have bought the old Kirkendall house, remodeled it and kept it—for her. "You bought this house nine years ago, after we were divorced, after I'd left Prospect. I don't understand."

"It was a crazy thing to do," he admitted. "But I thought that maybe someday…" He raked his hand through his hair and chuckled. "Hell, I don't know what

I thought. That by buying this house I was holding on to a little piece of you, I guess."

"How many rooms are there upstairs?" Christa asked.

"Four bedrooms and three baths."

"That's more than enough rooms for all of us. When you and Kate get married again, you'll share a room, of course. And I'll have my own room. And Nana will have her room. And there will be a guest bedroom. Or heck, maybe we'll have a baby. I always wanted a little brother or sister."

Kate and Trent stared at each other, totally amazed by Christa's exuberance.

"What if Trent and I don't remarry?" Kate asked. "What if I come back to Prospect and you and I and Brenda live here?"

Christa looked at Trent. "But if we're going to be a family, Trent has to live here, too. Right?"

"Are you saying that you want to come to Prospect to live?" Trent asked. "Do you want us to be your parents?"

"I guess. I mean, yes, I think that's what I want. But not if we have to live at Winston Hall."

"This can be your home," Trent told her. "And you can redo your room anyway you'd like. But it'll be up to Kate whether I live here with y'all or just visit every day."

Christa grabbed Kate's hand. "Please, Kate, tell him he can live here, too."

"Christa, honey…"

Christa reached out for Trent's hand. "I have a great idea, why don't we go get Nana and we all stay here for our visit."

"Would that make you happy?" Kate asked.

"Yes, it would be the very best birthday present."

"Then that's what we'll do." Kate looked to Trent. "Right?"

"Nothing would please me more." He wrapped one arm around Kate and the other around Christa. Both of them looked up at him and smiled.

Twelve

Winter turned into early spring. The days Christa spent with Kate in Prospect flew by, but the days Kate was on Dundee assignments and Christa in school in Sheffield seemed endless. Kate and Christa kept in touch by daily telephone conversations and she and Trent spoke often, too, their main topic of conversation always their daughter. She felt certain Trent wanted to ask her to remarry him, but she'd done everything to put him off, short of telling him she wouldn't go into a marriage only for the sake of their child. A part of her wanted to believe that Trent loved her and would want to remarry her regardless of whether Mary Kate had come back into their lives. But the insecure girl-from-the-wrong-side-of-the-tracks, who'd always felt so unworthy, had her doubts.

With Christa's spring break from school beginning, Brenda Farrell had arranged for them to arrive in

Prospect this Friday evening and stay for nine whole days. Kate could hardly wait. She had come into town the day before and spent the entire day today preparing the house on Madison for their guests' arrival. Trent had joined her for dinner last night and they'd ended the evening by making love. Each time they were together it became harder and harder to stop herself from telling him how much she loved him.

Before he'd left that morning, he'd made a request. "I'd like to stay here with you and Christa during this visit."

"You're welcome to stay, but you can't sleep with me," she'd told him, only halfway joking. "I don't think Brenda would approve. She's the old-fashioned type."

"I'll sleep on the porch if I have to," he said. "I just want to be here with you and our daughter. We've lost so many years. I don't want to lose another minute."

"Oh, Trent. Brenda told me that if this extended visit goes as well as the short weekend visits have gone, she thinks Christa will soon be ready for them to move here permanently."

When he'd hugged her, she'd sensed he didn't want to let her go, as if he was afraid he'd lose her. "If that's the case, don't you think we should make some decisions about our future."

"Not now, Trent. Let's wait and see how it goes."

She had put him off once again. But sooner or later she'd have to face the inevitable. It was only a matter of time before Trent proposed. And then she would have to decide if she could trust him completely, if she could believe he truly loved her.

"Where shall I put these, dear?" Aunt Mary Belle held a large floral arrangement, flowers from the Winston Hall spring garden.

"Those go in Brenda's room," Kate said.

"I think I'll suggest to Brenda that she should come over to Winston Hall and stay with me so that you and Trent can have some time alone with Christa."

Kate groaned. "I know you mean well, but please don't do that."

Mary Belle harrumphed. "Brenda needs to start letting go, just a little. You're the child's mother and unless Brenda allows Christa to bond with you—"

"Let's face it—my daughter may never think of me as her mother. She may always see Brenda in that role."

Mary Belle sighed, then turned to take the flowers into the guest bedroom Brenda Farrell would occupy. Kate returned to her chore—making Christa's bed with the new pale yellow bed linens she'd purchased in Atlanta. She'd found out recently that yellow was Christa's favorite color, so she'd made plans to add more of that color to this room.

"Where is everybody?" Trent called from downstairs.

"We're up here," she told him.

"I'll be on up as soon as I put the groceries away."

"Did you remember the Turtle Tracks ice cream?" Kate asked. "It's her favorite, you know."

"I got it. And the cereal she likes and the strawberry-flavored milk she prefers. You gave me specific instructions, honey. Stop worrying. Everything will be perfect."

"Everything will not be perfect until you two get married again," Mary Belle called out loud and clear.

Silence.

Say something, Trent. Please.

"I'll thank you to stay out of my business," Trent told his aunt.

Kate released her pent-up breath.

Mary Belle came into Christa's room and zeroed in on Kate. "Why won't you marry him?"

"I beg your pardon." Kate rearranged the decorative pillows on the four-poster bed.

"Don't play dumb with me. I know my nephew has been walking around with your engagement ring in his pocket for over a month now. Why haven't you said yes?"

"Trent has my engagement ring? Do you mean he kept my original ring, the one he gave me years ago?"

"That very ring. Half of Prospect is aware of the fact that Trent took your engagement ring and wedding band out of his safety-deposit box this past month."

Kate laughed spontaneously, finding great humor in the fact that a bank employee had spread the word about Trent's withdrawal from his safety-deposit box and that within a few days afterward half the town had known what he'd done. And wasn't it strange, Kate thought, that she didn't seem to mind at all. Once she had hated small-town gossip and the busybodies who generated it. Now she liked everything about Prospect, absolutely everything.

"Trent has not proposed," Kate told Mary Belle.

"He hasn't?"

"No, he hasn't."

"I find that odd."

"Why should you find—"

"Have you been discouraging him?"

Kate gave Mary Belle a withering glare.

"You have, haven't you?" Mary Belle huffed indignantly. "Why on earth would you do such a thing?"

"Why would Kate do what?" Trent asked from where he stood in the doorway to Christa's room.

Kate and Mary Beth gasped and jumped simultaneously.

"I'm going to hang a bell around your neck," his aunt told him.

"Pardon me. Did I interrupt private woman talk?"

"Yes, you did," Mary Belle said. "Kate, I'd very much like for y'all to come to lunch on Sunday, right after church."

"We'd be delighted, Aunt Mary Belle," Kate replied.

Trent looked from his aunt to Kate, his brow wrinkled, his gaze narrowed. "Aren't you two awfully chummy these days?"

"Kate, we'll finish our conversation at a later date. I must run. I have a dinner engagement with the other members of the museum's board of trustees and I shall need a good two hours to bathe and dress." She walked over to Kate, kissed her on the cheek, then did the same to Trent. "Give Christa my love and tell Brenda that there's a room at Winston Hall for her any time she'd like to take me up on my offer."

When his aunt walked out of the room, Trent eyed Kate questioningly. "What's that about—Brenda has a room at Winston Hall?"

"Oh, it's nothing. Just Aunt Mary Belle being Aunt Mary Belle."

Trent came up to Kate and slipped his arm around her, then kissed her on the mouth. When he lifted his head and smiled dreamily, she grinned back at him.

"Before Christa and Brenda arrive, there's something I want to ask you." He took her hands in his and led her out of the bedroom and into the hallway.

Don't propose to me now, she cried silently. *I'm not sure if I can say yes. Not yet.*

She gave him a pleading look.

He stuck his hand in his jacket pocket. Kate's heart stopped. He knelt on one knee.

"Oh, Trent."

"Kate…" He held up her engagement ring—a three-carat emerald cut stone. "You accepted this ring from me once before." He gazed up at her longingly. "I'm hoping you'll wear my ring again."

"I want—"

"Shh. Let me finish." He took her hand in his. "Kate, will you marry me. Again?"

Before she could utter a word, he slipped the ring on the third finger of her left hand. Kate stared at the sparkling diamond. She loved Trent with all her heart and soul and wanted to be his wife. Besides, remarrying him would be the best thing for Christa. It would make them a family. But that was the very reason she hesitated. She didn't want Trent to marry her because he thought it was the right thing to do for their daughter.

"Trent, why do you want to marry me?"

He stared at her, a puzzled expression darkening his face.

"Yoo-hoo," Brenda Farrell called out from downstairs. "We're here. Mary Belle let us in as she was leaving."

"Oh, God, it's Christa and Brenda," Kate said. "They're early."

"We're upstairs," Trent called. "We'll be right down."

When Kate headed toward the stairs, Trent grabbed her wrist to halt her. "Say yes now."

"Later."

She offered him an encouraging smile, then pulled free of his hold and raced down the stairs to greet Christa and Brenda. Trent came down only a second behind her. Kate skidded to a halt in the foyer, stopping herself only seconds before reaching out to Christa. More than anything she wanted to wrap her daughter in her arms and hug her for dear life. Although she and Trent had made amazing progress with Christa, a barrier still existed between them and their child. And they had agreed not to push her, to give her all the time she needed, to let her come to them when she was ready.

"Hi." Christa had Trent's wide-mouthed smile. "We left Sheffield early. School let out at noon and Nana had us all packed and ready to leave."

"Well, we're delighted y'all arrived early." Trent grinned at Christa, then turned to Brenda. "I'll bring in your bags."

"Just get Christa's bags," Brenda said.

Kate and Trent stared questioningly at her.

"I'm going to stay at Winston Hall with Mary Belle," Brenda explained. "I'll be close by and be able to see Christa every day."

Kate looked directly at her daughter. "Are you all right with those arrangements?"

"Oh, sure. Nana and I talked it over last night. She thinks I need to spend time with you two without her and I'm okay with it."

"Did Aunt Mary Belle have something to do with this?" Trent asked.

Brenda's lips curved into a how-ever-did-you-guess grin. "Don't be upset with her. She telephoned me earlier this week and made the suggestion. And she's right. I'm Christa's grandmother and nothing will change that fact. I'll always be close by when she needs me, but she has a mother and father now and y'all need to form a family bond."

Trent nodded. "Why don't y'all go on in while I get Christa's bags."

"I'm not staying," Brenda said. "Come on, Trent, I'll walk back to the car with you."

She leaned over and hugged Christa. "Behave yourself, young lady." She looked at Kate. "Do not let her get away with anything. She's a smart little cookie. She knows you and Trent will jump through hoops to pacify her."

"Ah, Nana, you're giving away all my secrets." Christa laughed.

"Are you hungry? Would you like a snack?" Kate asked her daughter as Trent opened the front door for Brenda and the two disappeared onto the front porch.

"Do you have any of those homemade oatmeal cookies?" Christa asked.

"I made a fresh batch this morning."

"Oh, Kate, thanks. I knew you would. You're the best."

Christa's smile warmed Kate's heart.

When Kate shoved open the kitchen door, Christa gasped. "Oh, my heavens, Kate, what is that on your finger?"

"What?" Damn, she was still wearing the three-carat diamond Trent had slipped on her finger. "Oh, that's the ring your father gave me when he asked me to marry him the first time."

"Are you two going to get married again?"

"Would you like that?"

"You know I would."

"We're talking about it," Kate said. "We haven't made a definite decision."

"If you do get married again, I could be the maid of honor, couldn't I?"

"Yes, of course, you could."

Oh, Trent, what am I going to do? I love you and

want to marry you. Nothing would please our daugh-
ter more. But you haven't said one word about loving
me. I need the words, Trent, I need the words.

The evening had been perfect, the kind Kate had once dreamed of having with her husband and daughter. With Trent and Mary Kate. And despite the years of separation and the fact that Christa was now their daughter's name, the three of them had shared a true family evening. Dinner together in the kitchen. Mother and daughter doing the dishes. Sitting on the front porch at sunset, despite it being slightly chilly. Watching Christa's favorite Friday night TV program while the three of them shared the sofa, Christa sitting between them.

When the mantel clock struck ten, Kate rose from the sofa and Trent used the remote control to turn off the television.

"Bedtime," Kate announced.

"You're going to follow Nana's instructions to the letter, aren't you?" Christa sighed dramatically.

"Nana knows best," Trent told her.

"Go on up and change into your new pajamas," Kate said. "I bought them in Atlanta and put them in the top drawer of your dresser this morning."

Christa jumped up and down. "Are they those yellow silk pajamas I wanted?"

"Could be."

"Oh, Kate, you *are* the very best." Christa came barreling toward Kate and threw her arms around her.

Kate thought she'd die from joy when her daughter hugged her fiercely, then released her and ran up the stairs. Trent came up behind Kate and pulled her back against his chest, then nuzzled her cheek with his.

"Good feeling, huh?"

"Great feeling." Kate turned around, right into Trent's arms. "Oh, Trent, I'm so happy."

"Me, too, honey. Me, too."

"I know we need to talk." She held up her ring finger. "About this. But could it wait until morning? I want to go up now and see Christa in her new pajamas and then I hope she'll let me stay with her so we can have some girl talk before she goes to sleep."

Trent kissed Kate quickly, then turned her and gave her a shove toward the stairs. She raced halfway up the steps, then paused, looked over her shoulder and blew her former husband a kiss.

"I love you," she mouthed the words and waited for his response.

He shut his eyes for a brief moment, an odd expression on his face. When he opened his eyes again, he smiled at her, but didn't say anything. *Did that mean he didn't love her? Dammit Trent, am I supposed to be able to read your mind?*

Kate lay awake, torn between wanting to go to Trent and wishing he would come to her. She'd been the one who had decided they shouldn't share a bedroom while Christa and Brenda were in the house with them. But tonight was different. First of all, Brenda wasn't here. And secondly, Trent had proposed. She was wearing an engagement ring.

But you haven't said yes, she reminded herself.

Was she allowing three little words to keep her from accepting, from grabbing everything she'd ever wanted and holding on tight? What did it matter that Trent hadn't told her he loved her. He'd shown her in countless ways. Not only did he make her feel loved and cherished every time they made love, but he'd done everything in his power to give her whatever she wanted. He'd let her have her way about their relationship and about dealing with Christa and Brenda and even Aunt Mary Belle.

And don't forget that he bought this house nine years ago—bought it in the hopes you'd come back to him. And he kept it, remodeled it and held on to it all this time. And he gave it to you—in writing, putting the deed in your name.

How much more did a man have to do to prove his love?

Kate slipped out of bed, picked up her satin robe and put it on. Just as she headed for the door, she heard a soft rapping.

"Kate," Trent whispered her name.

She opened the door to him. He stood there in the dark hallway, wearing his pajama bottoms and silk robe, loosely belted. He looked as if he'd gotten no more sleep than she had.

"I was coming to you," she told him.

"Christa is sound asleep. I peeked in on her on my way to your room."

"Couldn't you wait till morning to find out my answer?" she said teasingly.

"I can wait for your answer." He shut the door behind him, then reached out and pulled her up against him, enfolding her securely in his embrace. "But I can't wait until morning to make love to you."

"I feel the same way." Rising on tiptoe, she draped her arms around his neck and kissed him.

That was all it took for him to lose control. His mouth devoured hers and his hands went crazy, rubbing, caressing, massaging her back, her hips, her buttocks.

She gripped his wide shoulders as he deepened the kiss and when his sex thumped against her belly, she yanked off his robe and tossed it to the floor. Within minutes, he'd stripped her, then he discarded his pajama bottoms. They tumbled together onto her bed, touching and tasting each other, their bodies eager to join. She took the dominant position, mounting him, bringing him fully inside her, to the hilt. And then she began a fast, frantic pace, wanting him desperately. Needing him. Loving him. Always. He clasped her hips and urged her into a frenetic rhythm. Hard and fast. Hot and wet. They went at each other as if their very lives depended on this single mating.

Trent grunted. Once. Twice. And then he came.

Kate's own climax came on the heels of his, fast and furious. Pleasure almost beyond bearing. She melted into him, their sex-damp bodies sticky and hot. He stroked her buttocks as she kissed his neck.

"Kate. Kate…"

"I love you, Trent."

"I—"

The scream filled the entire house, as if the child's voice was magnified a thousand-fold. Kate shot straight up, her heart racing maddeningly. Oh my God, it was Christa!

"It's Christa," Kate told him as she got up, found her robe on the floor and slipped into it.

"She's crying. Listen." Trent followed Kate's lead and put on his robe, too.

"She must be having a nightmare."

Kate ran out into the hall and straight to Christa's bedroom. Trent came in right behind her. She rushed over to the bed where Christa thrashed about, moaning and groaning and clawing at the air. Acting purely on instinct, Kate crawled into bed with her child, pulled her into her arms and held her close.

"It's okay, baby, Mama's here," Kate said as she caressed Christa's head and neck and back. "You're safe my darling. No one can hurt you."

Trent stood beside the bed. Springtime moonlight poured through the windows, filtered only by the delicate white lace curtains. His gaze connected with Kate's and they exchanged concerned looks.

The more Kate petted Christa, the tighter she clung to Kate and the calmer she became until finally she quieted. Her eyelids fluttered. Kate kissed her forehead.

"That's it my sweet baby, rest. Mama's here and I'll never let anything or anyone hurt you ever again."

Christa opened her eyes and looked right at Kate. "I had a terrible dream."

"That's all it was, sweetheart. Just a dream. You're fine now."

"I dreamed that we were all together, living here in this house and we were so happy." Christa looked over Kate's shoulder and reached her hand out toward Trent. "Daddy?"

Kate's heart caught in her throat.

"Daddy, this terrible person tried to take me away, but you and Mama stopped him." Christa laid her head on Kate's shoulder. "Daddy fought him and saved me. And you grabbed me and held me, Mama, and told me you loved me."

Tears poured down Kate's cheeks. The joy bursting inside her hurt with the most intense pleasure-pain she'd ever known. *Thank you, God, thank you.* Christa had called her Mama. And she'd called Trent Daddy.

Trent leaned over the bed and wrapped his arms around Kate and Christa. "We both love you," he said.

"Your mother and I love you more than anything, just like we love each other. One of the reasons I love you so much is because you're half mine and half your mama's. And you're special, Christa, because you're you."

Kate reached up and caressed Trent's cheek. "The answer is yes," she told him.

He kissed Kate's forehead. Christa lifted her head from Kate's shoulder and said, "You can do better than that, can't you, Daddy?"

"Yes, I can, young lady, but not tonight. Tomorrow we'll celebrate properly and I'll give Kate a kiss that will knock her socks off. But for now, we all need to get some sleep. We've just been through quite an ordeal."

Trent turned to leave the bedroom.

"Don't go," Christa cried.

"All right, I'll stay." Trent walked across the room and sat in one of the two floral chintz lounge chairs flanking a small tea table. "I'll keep watch from here the rest of the night. Now, you two girls go to sleep."

Christa tugged on Kate's hands. "Sleep with me tonight, okay?"

"Okay." Kate lay down beside her daughter, then pulled the covers over them up to their shoulders.

Christa snuggled against Kate and whispered, "You're going to marry Daddy again, aren't you, Mama?"

"Yes, I am." Kate hugged Christa.

"And I'm going to be your maid of honor, right?"

"Right?"

"And I'm going to be the luckiest man in the world," Trent called from across the room.

"We're all three lucky," Kate said. "We're a real family again."

At long last.

Epilogue

"They're here," Christa Winston called out to her nana and aunt Mary Belle, then she rushed off the porch and down the brick sidewalk toward her mother and father who were just getting out of Trent's Bentley.

Kate opened her arms as Christa flew toward her.

After giving her mother a hug, Christa said, "May I carry one of them?"

Trent opened the car's back door and looked inside, then smiled at Christa. "Take your pick. Do you want Bay or Belle?"

"Give me Belle," thirteen-year old Christa said. "She and I will have to stick together, being sisters and all."

Trent removed the infant carrier from the back seat and handed his younger daughter to her big sister. "We think she looks just like you did when you were a baby."

"Which means she's a living doll, right Daddy?" Christa beamed happily as she accepted the carrier and headed up the sidewalk. "You should see your nursery, young lady. Mama and I went all out decorating it. Your side of the room is all pink and white. And I chose all your dolls and stuffed animals myself. We let Daddy pick out things for Bay, since he's a boy. He'll probably play football and baseball. But I'll teach you to play soccer and softball. I'm on both teams, you know."

Trent lifted his son's carrier from the car, then reached out and put his arm around Kate. "Miracles do happen, don't they, honey?"

"Absolutely. We are living proof of that."

"Hurry up, you two," Aunt Mary Belle fussed as she came toward them. "You do not want to keep that baby out in this hot July sun another minute. It's enough to give me a heat stroke. Ninety-five in the shade today. That's what the weather forecaster said."

Christa took Belle inside, then Brenda and Mary Belle followed. Kate held open the door for Trent and went in behind him and Bay. Kate gasped as they entered the foyer. Blue and pink streamers hung from the crown molding and draped the staircase. Baskets of fresh flowers—in pale baby pastels—had been situated in every corner of the foyer. Kate saw plainly Aunt Mary Belle's extravagant hand mixed with Christa's youthful exuberance in the celebratory displays.

The entire assembly treaded upstairs, straight to the nursery. The room, a pale cream, boasted a hand-painted mural, and had been decorated in shades of light pink, blue, yellow and green. The furniture for both babies was a rich mahogany—the baby beds, chests, dressing tables and rocking chairs. Trenton Bayard Winston V's bed was an identical Genny Lind style to his sister's except hers had a white-eyelet-lace canopy. Where Bay had his father's brown hair and mother's blue eyes, Brenda Belle Winston was her older sister's look-alike, with Trent's brown eyes and Kate's blond hair.

After removing both sleeping infants from their carriers and placing them in their beds, Christa and the adults stood watching the little ones, in awe of the miracle before them.

"Babies are so amazing, aren't they?" Brenda said. "I'd hoped to have more children after Rick, but it wasn't meant to be." She put her arm around Christa. "But God blessed me with this young lady."

"And now you have two more grandchildren." Christa looked from her mother to her father. "Isn't that right?"

"Absolutely," Kate said.

"And I'll teach them to call you Nana, just like I do," Christa told her.

"Christa, I'm not sure—"

"Of course, they'll call you Nana." Kate smiled at Brenda. "You and Aunt Mary Belle will share the honor of being their grandmother, just as y'all do with Christa."

"I've got to phone Shelly and Alexa and tell them they can come over and see our babies." Christa galloped out of the nursery, then called back to her parents, "Is it all right for them to come over in about an hour?"

"An hour should be fine," Trent replied, then draped his arm around Kate's shoulders. "Now, Mrs. Winston, I think it's time for you to lie down for a while. You've had a busy day today, not to mention the fact you just gave birth to twins only a few days ago."

"Brenda and I will go downstairs and see to lunch and field any phone calls." Mary Belle ushered Brenda from the nursery.

Trent and Kate heard the two talking like magpies as they went up the hall and down the stairs. Christa's nana and her aunt Mary Belle had become fast friends and both seemed to greatly enjoy living together at Winston Hall. Mary Belle had gotten Brenda involved in all her clubs and civic organizations and you seldom saw one of them without the other.

While the ladies kept busy and happy blocks away at the old family manor, Trent, Kate and Christa lived what Kate thought of as a fairly normal life here on Madison in their homey old house, with a swing on the front porch and a white picket fence. Last year Kate had thought she couldn't be happier, that she had everything her heart desired. That was until she discovered she was pregnant—at thirty-six—with twins.

Trent marched Kate into their bedroom and all but forced her to take off her shoes and lie down. "Rest while you can," he told her. He kissed her forehead, then turned to leave.

"Stay with me."

"You won't rest if I'm here."

"I won't rest if you're not."

"Okay, but no hanky-panky," Trent said jokingly as he got in bed with her and sat, his back against the headboard.

"We'll save the hanky-panky for a few weeks." She snuggled up against him, placing her head in his lap. "For now, I'll settle for some TLC. Lots and lots of TLC."

"Ah, honey, you're going to get plenty of tender loving care. Now and for the rest of our lives." He tenderly stroked her head, threading his fingers through her hair. "I love you, Kate. I love you so much it hurts."

She sighed. "And I love you the very same way."

Life didn't get any better than this. After years of loneliness and heartache, Kate and Trent had been given a precious gift—a second chance for a happy life as husband and wife. And as parents.

* * * * *

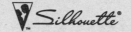

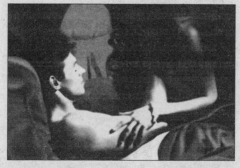

COMING NEXT MONTH

#1603 THE ENEMY'S DAUGHTER—Anne Marie Winston
Dynasties: The Danforths
Selene Van Gelder and Adam Danforth could not resist their deep attraction, despite the fact that their fathers were enemies. When their covert affair was leaked to the press, they each had to face the truth about their feelings. Would the feud between their families keep them apart—or was their love strong enough to overcome anything?

#1604 BRANDED—Annette Broadrick
The Crenshaws of Texas
When rancher Jake Crenshaw suddenly became a single dad, he asked Ashley Sullivan to temporarily care for his daughter. Ashley had harbored a big childhood crush on blond-haired Jake and her feelings were quickly reawakened. Now Ashley was in Jake's house—and sharing his bed—but where could this affair of convenience lead…?

#1605 MEETING AT MIDNIGHT—Eileen Wilks
Mantalk
Mysterious Seely Jones immediately mesmerized Ben McClain. He tried his best to pry into her deep, dark secrets but Seely held on tight to what he wanted. Ben kept up his hot pursuit, but would what he sought fan his flaming desire or extinguish his passion?

#1606 UNMASKING THE MAVERICK PRINCE—Kristi Gold
The Royal Wager
Never one for matrimony, Mitchell Edward Warner III didn't expect to lose a wager that he wouldn't marry for ten years. But when journalist Victoria Barnet set her sights on convincing blue-eyed Mitch to take his vows in exchange for a lifetime of passionate, wedded bliss, this sexy son of a senator started to reconsider.…

#1607 A BED OF SAND—Laura Wright
Neither Rita Thompson nor her gorgeous boss, Sheikh Sakir Ibn Yousef Al-Nayhal, meant for their mock marriage to go beyond business. She needed a groom to reunite her family, and he needed a bride to return to his homeland. Yet fictitious love soon turned into real passion and Rita couldn't resist her tall, dark and handsome desert prince.

#1608 THE FIRE STILL BURNS—Roxanne St. Claire
Competing architects Colin McGrath and Grace Harrington came from two different worlds. But when forced into close quarters for a design competition, it was more than blueprints that evoked their passion, and pretty soon Grace found herself falling for her hot and sexy rival.…

SDCNM0804